THE UNLUCKY COLLIE CAPER

THE UNLUCKY COLLIE CAPER

Book One
in
The Jennifer Gray
Veterinarian Mystery
Series

•

GEORGETTE LIVINGSTON

AVALON BOOKS
THOMAS BOUREGY AND COMPANY, INC.
401 LAFAYETTE STREET
NEW YORK, NEW YORK 10003

PRINTED IN THE UNITED STATES OF AMERICA
ON ACID-FREE PAPER
BY HADDON CRAFTSMEN, SCRANTON, PENNSYLVANIA

For Bonnie, Cindy, Melody, Mike and Jay—
for all that you are, and all that you mean to me.

Chapter One

On a little rise covered with wildflowers, Jennifer Gray sat astride her chestnut mare Tassie and lifted her face to the late-morning sun. The rays shimmered down on the fertile valley, where fields of corn grew high and lion-colored grasses rippled in the breeze. To the north, cattle grazed content-edly against a backdrop of purple-hued pla-teaus that stretched for miles. It was God's country, and she had missed it more than she'd ever thought possible. Especially this extraordinary spot that she had always thought of as a tiny corner of heaven. Not that she hadn't come home to visit during

1

the six years it had taken to get her degree in veterinary medicine, but Michigan State University was many miles away from Calico, Nebraska, and her vacations had always been brief. Now, she was home to stay, she was working with Ben Copeland as his veterinary assistant, and it was like a dream come true. Ben said he was grooming her to take over his practice because he planned to retire soon, but she knew it was a lot more involved than that. She needed much more experience before he could walk away comfortably, and she needed to gain the confidence of the community, to prove to the skeptics that she was capable of caring for their animals. Their biggest concern, of course, was the fact she was a woman. Or maybe it went even deeper than that. She was still "little Jennifer Gray" to most of them—the tomboy on the bright-red bicycle, with blond pigtails flying in the breeze. The little girl who, after her parents' fatal automobile accident, had gone to live with her widowed grandfather, Wesley Gray, pastor of the Calico Christian Church. She had also been the little girl who had a way with animals, and always seemed to have a "patient" somewhere around the house.

Her grandfather knew she was going to be a veterinarian the day she brought home the injured crow. He'd watched her splint its broken wing with Popsicle sticks, and told her she had a special gift, a calling. But it wasn't until she'd started high school that he told her about the trust fund left to her by her parents. The choice was hers, of course, but if she wanted to go to college and veterinary school, there was more than enough money. She had cried that day, feeling so close to her mother and father, and knowing how much they had loved her. It had also been the day she had made her decision. And she'd never regretted it.

Tassie nickered softly and twitched her ears. Jennifer gave the mare a loving pat, and smiled. "I know, sweet lady. I've missed you too. And I promise—no matter how busy I am, or how involved my life gets, I'll always find the time to be with you, and share this special place."

She urged the horse down the trail, but not before taking one last look at the tapestry of colors spread out before them. She was home where she belonged, and hugged her happiness close.

The white clapboard house sat beside the steepled church, but far enough back to allow for a lovely, front-yard garden. Most of it was Emma's doing, though Jennifer's grandfather had a green thumb too, and insisted on taking some of the credit. "The tomatoes are mine," he'd say. "And the radishes. Have you ever seen radishes that big or firm?"

Emma Morrison, who had been his housekeeper for years, would put her hands on her plump hips and announce, "Ah, but have you ever seen bigger sunflowers? And who grows the tallest snapdragons in town?"

"You can't eat snapdragons," Wes would mutter.

"And you can't cut bouquets of tomatoes and radishes for the dining-room table," Emma would spout back.

It wasn't that Emma didn't appreciate the bounty of vegetables right at her fingertips, or that her grandfather didn't appreciate the colorful display of freshly picked flowers whos fragrance would waft through the house all summer. They simply enjoyed bickering.

Jennifer could hear them arguing now, as she made her way along the tree-lined walkway. She could also smell chicken soup, and her grandfather *hated* chicken soup. He said the only thing it was good for was a cold, and even then he had to be nearly delirious with a fever before he would allow what he considered "Emma's anemic dishwater" to pass between his lips.

"Chicken soup and a glass of milk," Emma was saying as Jennifer walked into the sun-splashed kitchen. "It's a fitting lunch even on a summer day, Mr. Wes. Besides, that girl is too thin. She needs tender loving care and good food to put some meat on her bones!"

Emma looked up, saw Jennifer, and flushed. "Well, it's true."

Wes was poking around in the cupboards, then turned and scowled. "You hear that, Jennifer? She thinks she's going to put meat on your bones with a scrawny chicken." He noted the color in her cheeks, the brightness in her eyes, and the scowl turned into a smile. "I take it you had a good ride?"

"I had a wonderful ride, and chicken soup sounds great."

Wes pulled out a jar of peanut butter, and grumbled under his breath.

Jennifer sat down at the table, and watched the two people she loved most in all the world. Emma, at sixty-five, didn't have a strand of gray in her frizzy brown hair. Jennifer's grandfather, on the other hand, had a head of snow-white hair. He had pink cheeks too, and bright blue eyes, and could have passed for Santa Claus if he had a beard. Emma claimed his hair was white because he worried too much about the town and his congregation. *He* claimed if he didn't worry, who would? Today, life was hard, harder than it should be, and nobody had time for anything but work. Everybody always seemed to be in a hurry, barely taking the time to say hello or smile, and that was what happened when a town got too big for its britches. Even the old boys, long retired, who used to sit on the bench at Grover's Corner and pass the time of day, were busily at work building the senior citizens' center on a piece of land coughed up by Elmer Dodd, who owned the local dairy. Land, according to Wes, that wasn't fit to raise scrawny chickens.

Jennifer understood how her grandfather felt. Before she'd gone off to college, Calico had been a small Nebraska town where time stood still. A town rich in history, where the faces, with the exception of growing older, were always the same. Now, there was a shopping mall east of town, and a three-story hospital on the other side of the White River bridge. New businesses had popped up everywhere, and sometimes you had to walk three blocks before you would see a familiar face. It was called progress and, good or bad, it had come to stay.

Jennifer watched her grandfather make a peanut butter sandwich and said, ''Max has taken good care of Tassie, even though business seems to be booming. He's had to hire more help, and build additional stalls.''

Wes grunted. ''Did he tell you he might have to move the stable? We had a town meeting a few weeks before you came home. Most folks seem to think the stable is too close to the new park. It didn't take much for them to speak up. Apparently they feel that picnics and horse manure aren't compatible.''

''No, he didn't tell me, though he did seem preoccupied. Why did they have to put the park so close to the stable? And did we really need another park? We have them all over town, and the green belt along the river is full of picnic areas.''

''Yeah, well, some of those parks 'all over town' are going to be turned into commercial property. The council says we need more room for businesses. I say we should all thank God for giving us this town, and if we're not careful, we're going to ruin it. I know that without a certain amount of progress a town can die, but too much can turn it into something it was never meant to be.''

He looked at his watch. ''Aren't you supposed to go to work this afternoon?''

''Not until two. Ben had a doctor's appointment at one.''

''And he doesn't think you can run the clinic without him?''

''More than likely he knows how most

people feel,'' Emma muttered, dishing up a bowl of chicken soup. She placed it in front of Jennifer, and shook her head. ''I was in the market the other day, and overheard Penelope Davis tell Emily Wilcox that one of her cats was ailing, but there was no way she was going to let 'that Gray girl' within ten feet of it. I stepped right up and asked her what was she going to do when Ben Copeland retires? She looked down her nose at me and said Elmer Dodd has a nephew who's a big-time vet in Omaha, and he's already talked to him about moving to Calico.''

''Competition never hurt anybody,'' Jennifer said easily, though it wasn't what she was thinking. Competition like that, before she could establish herself as a competent vet, would be disastrous.

''That's the spirit,'' Wes said, giving his granddaughter a wink. ''Show 'em what you're made of. Now, I have to go. I have a wedding on Saturday, and I'm meeting with both sets of parents in an hour. They're giving the reception in the church social hall, and want to make sure it will hold fifty people.''

"Didn't you tell them it will hold a hundred and fifty people?" Jennifer asked.

"Sure I did. *And* the Thompsons told them, but the Millers are new in town, and want to see the facilities with their own eyes."

"Thompsons? Are you telling me Amy Thompson is getting married?" Jennifer was incredulous.

Wes grinned. "She sure is. I know, when you went off to college, she had braces on her teeth and a chip on her shoulder. I remember the day you brought her home like one of your wounded animals because she was threatening to run away, and you thought I could help. She sat right where you're sitting, and said she was never, *ever* going to get married. Her parents were having marital difficulties at the time, if you recall, and she was pretty unhappy. Well, everything changed after the parents got some counseling. They reconciled their differences and became a family again—a strong family, and the change in Amy was a wonderful sight to see."

Jennifer sighed. "So little Amy Thompson is getting married. It makes me feel ancient, and as though I've been away forever.''

"Six years is a long time," Emma reasoned. "And you've changed too. You went away a girl, and now you're a young woman."

Wes tweaked Jennifer's cheek. "And a very pretty young woman. Enjoy the afternoon, sweetheart. I'll see you at dinner."

After her grandfather had gone, Jennifer finished the bowl of chicken soup and headed for the clinic, wondering if Ben Copeland knew about Elmer Dodd's nephew in Omaha.

The clinic was on East Front Street, near the cemetery, and it was a good location—close to town, yet far enough away so nobody would be bothered by barking dogs. She and Ben Copeland handled large animals too, which meant a certain amount of traveling, because nobody was expected to bring a horse or a cow to the clinic. There were two teenage helpers who worked after school and during the summer months. Although their jobs were varied, most of it was cleanup, but the boys didn't care. They loved animals, and their help was invaluable.

Jennifer parked her Jeep Cherokee under a stand of maple trees and walked in the back door, prepared to ask Ben about the vet in Omaha. But when she found him bending over a collie stretched out on an examining table, nothing seemed to matter but the concern and frustration on his weathered face—or the fact that the collie looked near death. Even its gorgeous, golden-brown and white coat was limp and lifeless. Its dark-brown eyes were open but staring, and occasionally a limb would twitch.

"So much for my doctor's appointment," Ben muttered. "Rat poison, I would suspect. Probably strychnine. At least he's showing all the classic symptoms—dilated pupils, twitching, and stiff neck muscles. When the owner called, I told her to induce vomiting with hydrogen peroxide, follow it with a strong dose of tea, and then bring him into the clinic. I had to talk her through it because she was hysterical. Now, all we can do is wait."

"Did you inject a contra-active agent and wash out the stomach and intestines?" Jennifer asked.

A smile played at the corners of his mouth. "I sure did. Can you tell me what's supposed to happen next?"

"He'll either recover or go into convulsions. His limbs will become rigid, and the neck will bend up backward. If that happens, we've lost him," she said sadly.

"Good girl. What about putting liquid into his mouth?"

Jennifer shook her head. "It would more than likely go into his lungs and cause foreign-body pneumonia." She ran a hand through the collie's thick coat. "How did it happen, Ben?"

"The owner was too upset to tell me. Why don't you go talk to her? She's in the waiting room, and she's still hysterical. Her name is Pam Aldrich."

"Aldrich. Any relation to Richard Aldrich, the rancher?"

"His wife. They met while he was on vacation back East. At least that's what I heard. They've been married about a year."

Jennifer walked down the hall and into the waiting room, and her heart twisted at the sight of the distraught woman. She was pretty and petite, but her hair was wild, her clothes were askew, and her face was awash with tears.

"Mrs. Aldrich," Jennifer began, "I'd like to talk to you about your dog—"

The woman clasped her hands together. "How is he? Is he . . . okay?"

Jennifer sat down beside the woman, and tried for a smile. "It's too soon to tell. I'm Jennifer Gray, Dr. Copeland's assistant. What's your dog's name?"

"Bart."

"It would really help us if you could give us some idea of how much poison Bart ingested."

The woman rocked back and forth. "It was in the hamburger."

"In the hamburger?" Jennifer asked incredulously. "I don't understand."

"I was going to broil a hamburger patty to eat with an egg. I took the meat out of the refrigerator and made a patty. But before I could get it under the broiler, it fell to the floor. Bart was right there, and gobbled it down . . . I scolded him, of course, and made a second patty. But before I could get *it* cooked, the phone rang. It was my sister in Boston. We talked for a few minutes, and then Bart began staggering around and acting strange. I couldn't locate my husband, and that's when I called Dr. Copeland. He asked me to describe the symptoms, and told me what to do. He told me Bart had been poisoned. . . . He said it was some type of rat poison—probably strychnine. Don't you see, Miss Gray? The poison was in the hamburger, and it was meant for me!''

Jennifer was not only stunned by the woman's words, she was speechless. After an awkward pause, she finally said, ''Surely not. I know you're upset, but there must be some other explanation. Strychnine is a readily available rat poison, along with arsenic, ANTU and thallium. Perhaps your dog ingested a dead rat that had been poisoned, and eating the hamburger patty was only a coincidence.''

The woman ran a shaky hand through her titian-colored hair. ''Perhaps. You'll have to forgive me, but this has been so upsetting . . .''

''Of course, but if you truly believe someone tried to poison you, you can call the authorities and have the hamburger analyzed.''

Pam shook her head vigorously. ''No . . . no, I couldn't do that. Please forget what I told you, Miss Gray. I'm sure it happened just the way you said—Bart found a poisoned rat.''

''What did you do with the rest of the hamburger?''

''Why, I left it on the counter . . . no, I threw it in the garbage. Yes, that's what I did.''

''You mentioned you couldn't locate your husband.''

Pam cast her eyes downward. ''He was out on the ranch somewhere.''

''Then he still has the ranch south of town?''

The woman pursed her lips. ''You know my husband?''

''No, I don't know him personally, but I knew his . . .'' It was Jennifer's turn to cast her eyes downward. *Be sure your brain is*

engaged before your mouth is in motion.
She remembered her grandfather's words
from years ago, when she'd had a habit of
putting her foot in her mouth. Unfortunately, she hadn't been able to completely
master such self-control.

"You knew his first wife, Mary." Pam
Aldrich said tonelessly.

Jennifer took a deep breath. Mary had
been Richard Aldrich's *third* wife, but apparently he hadn't bothered to let Pam in
on that little piece of information.

"Well, yes," Jennifer said, feeling her
ears burn with the lie. "I'm sorry, Mrs. Aldrich. I was out of line."

Pam waved a hand. "It doesn't matter.
Nothing matters if Bart doesn't pull
through."

Jennifer gave the woman a comforting
pat on the arm. "He's in good hands, Mrs.
Aldrich, but it wouldn't hurt to say a little
prayer. Now, if you'll excuse me . . ."

Tears shimmered in Pam's eyes. "Yes,
yes—please go and do what you can to
help poor Bart."

Jennifer walked into the emergency examining room, and let out her breath in one

big poof. "She says the poison was in the hamburger, and it was meant for her," she announced.

Ben took the stethoscope out of his ears, and ran a hand through his gray, wiry hair. "She said *what?*"

"She seems to think somebody is trying to kill her. Or at least that's the impression I got."

"But that's crazy."

"That's what I thought, until she retracted her statement and decided to shine it off. It was like she realized what she'd said, and tried to cover it up. How well do you know Richard Aldrich?"

"Well enough to know I don't like him. One of his ranch hands doubles as a vet. That's because Aldrich doesn't trust me. He calls me a small-town hick, and says no hick is gonna tend to his animals."

"And does this ranch hand have a licence to practice veterinary medicine?" Jennifer asked pointedly.

He says he does, but I have my doubts. He came by the clinic a couple of months ago, asking me all kinds of questions— questions he should have known the answers to. Then he said, 'I'd appreciate it if we could keep this little visit between us.' ''

''What's his name?''

''Goes by Tyler. Didn't give me a last name, or maybe that *is* his last name.''

The collie seemed to be resting comfortably, and it was a good sign. ''I wonder why Pam Aldrich didn't ask Tyler for help. If he's on the ranch . . .'' Jennifer mused.

''Maybe she knows the truth about his lack of expertise.''

''Which also makes me wonder why a man like Richard Aldrich would put his cattle at risk, using a man like that. We're talking about hundreds of thousands of dollars.''

''Not any more. His herd is down to a paltry few. Sold most of them last year.''

''Before he married Pam?''

''Yeah. Rumor had it he was nearly broke, but nobody could figure out why. And nobody was close enough to him to ask. He's been living in Calico nearly fifteen years, and he's still a stranger.''

''I knew his last wife,'' Jennifer said thoughtfully. ''I met her the summer before

I went away to college. I had Tassie out for a run, and I passed her on the trail. She was riding a chestnut gelding, and I noticed the horse first, because it was lathered and breathing hard. And then I noticed Mary. Her face was pale, and she was drooping in the saddle. At first I thought it was heat-stroke, but by the time I got her off the horse and into the shade, I realized she was ill. She was ice-cold and trembling. I knew it was Aldrich's new wife, because I'd seen them in town together. I was frantic, Ben. I was trying to decide if I should go to town for help or to the ranch, when Aldrich rode up, looking dark and angry and totally out of sorts. He didn't acknowledge me at all. He simply scooped up his wife, plopped her on her horse, and muttered something about how she'd better hang on because he sure wasn't going to carry her. I was left swallowing his dust. When I went home and told Grandfather, he said her name was Mary, she was from Bismarck, North Dakota, and he'd heard she'd been ill for months. Some people were even saying she was mentally disturbed. That was also the day I found out Mary was his third wife.

He'd been married two times before he moved to Calico. I tried to forget about it, but I couldn't get Mary out of my mind. I was really worried about her. A week later, I rode out to the ranch and found her sitting on a bench under a peachleaf willow. She was still pale, but her smile was wonderful. And she actually remembered me. She said her husband was out of town on business, and offered me a cup of tea. I declined, but we spent an hour chatting. I asked her about her illness, and she said she had some kind of a bug she couldn't shake. Everything was great until it was time to leave, and I told her I'd stop by again. She got a wild look in her eyes and told me it wasn't a good idea. She said her husband didn't take kindly to company, and she didn't want to make him angry.

"I went away to college that fall, and when I came home for Christmas vacation, I heard she had passed away."

"Maybe she had a terminal illness," Ben reasoned.

"Maybe, but you know what's really strange? Pam Aldrich knows about Mary, but thinks she was Richard's first wife. She doesn't know about the other two.''

''She told you that?''

''In a roundabout way.

''Maybe he found it was easier to put the past behind him.''

Jennifer shrugged, but her thoughts were on hamburger laced with strychnine, and the look in Pam Aldrich's eyes. It was the same look she had seen in Mary's eyes, and there was only one word to describe it . . . fear.

Chapter Two

By four o'clock that afternoon, they had performed surgery on a female cat with a bowel obstruction, patched up a ten-month-old male German shepherd that had gotten into a scuffle with a littermate, and had listened to Kyle Wallace list numerous reasons why he had to quit his job. Bobby Kanter stood on one foot and then the other, listening to his friend, and then finally admitted he was going to quit too. They liked the work, they said, but it was taking up too much of their summer. Ben gave them a ten-minute lecture about responsibility before he kicked them out.

23

And he was still muttering "Kids!" when he called *The Calico Review* to place a help-wanted ad.

Jennifer listened to him argue with the circulation department about the cost of the ad. She realized he wasn't only upset, he was overly tired. The minute he hung up, she told him to take a break. He gave her a grateful smile, and headed for the door.

An hour later, Jennifer found him sitting on a bench in the small flower garden behind the clinic, staring off into space. She sat down beside him and handed him a cup of coffee. "I sent Pam Aldrich home. She was exhausted, and now that the collie is going to pull through . . . Oh, and I called the cat's owners, to tell them the surgery was a success. I also warned them about keeping rubber bands picked up. They had a hard time believing one little rubber band could do so much damage to a cat's intestines."

Ben patted Jennifer's hand. "And I've been trying to figure out how I ever got along without you."

Jennifer grinned. "Flattery will get you everywhere."

"Yeah, well, it might not after you have to do double duty. Mopping the floor and hosing down the kennel won't put a smile on your face. I swear, when I was sixteen, I worked my fingers to the bone, trying to save enough money for college. The kids today have it too easy. For sure, they don't have any direction. No motivation."

"You can't lump all the kids together, Ben. Not all of them are irresponsible. And somebody will answer the ad. You'll see."

He sighed. "I wish I had your optimism. I suppose I should get something to eat if I'm going to have to keep an eye on the collie and cat all night."

"I've already made the arrangements, Ben. I called Grandfather and told him I'll be working until two A.M. You can relieve me then."

Ben ran his fingers over his eyes. "But you have to eat."

"I'll order a pizza. I know—I was the first to complain when I heard about all the fast-food places in town, but I have to admit, sometimes they come in handy. Oh, and I called your wife, and told her you were on your way home. She was delighted. She said she was going right into the kitchen and fix your favorite dinner.''

''Spaghetti?''

''With garlic bread.''

Ben gave her a lopsided grin. ''Guess it's out of my hands, huh?''

''You betcha. So go enjoy your dinner and some quiet time with Irene, but don't forget to get some sleep.''

He gave her a little salute, and headed for his car.

Jennifer watched Ben drive off, trying to dispel the sense of foreboding she felt. She didn't like the droop to his shoulders, or the gray cast of his skin. She made a mental note to remind him to reschedule his doctor's appointment, and then walked into the clinic to face the long evening ahead.

It was almost ten o'clock when Jennifer heard the pounding on the front door. Thinking it was an emergency, she hurried to open it, and then gasped. Richard Aldrich loomed in the doorway, scowling down at her. ''I've come to get my dog,'' he muttered, pushing his way into the waiting room.

Jennifer managed to take a stand in front of him, and returned his scowl. "Your dog almost died, Mr. Aldrich, and he's in no condition to be released."

He stared down at her, as though he were remembering some other time, some other place. The muscles worked spasmodically along his jawline. "Yeah, well, that's your opinion. I'm going to take him home, and there isn't one blessed thing you can do about it."

Jennifer squared her shoulders. "No, there isn't, but I can tell you you're making a big mistake."

He took another step. "I have my own vet, and he can see to Bart's needs."

"Bart is very weak. You'll have to carry him . . ."

The man shrugged.

Jennifer's thoughts were like a kaleidoscope in her head, opening and closing, and taking different shapes. She couldn't stop him, but she *could* call Sheriff Cody. She took a deep breath. Right, and then what? There was no way the sheriff was going to send out a patrol car because of a dog. But maybe with some quick thinking . . .

Jennifer was five-foot-seven, and although she was on the thin side, she was wiry and strong. She worked out every morning to maintain the kind of muscle tone it took to perform her duties. She never knew when she might have to restrain or subdue a large animal. And although Richard Aldrich was at least six-two, and massive, he didn't frighten her. Nor would she allow him to intimidate her. Bart's well-being was all that mattered.

She placed a finger against the man's chest, and pushed. "I think you had better leave, Mr. Aldrich. Your dog was poisoned, and the proper authorities have been notified. Until an investigation can be conducted . . . ''

His cheeks puffed up. "You're nuts!"

"What I am is a competent veterinarian, and you are interfering with my patient."

"It's just a lousy dog," he grumbled.

Jennifer felt anger touch every nerve ending in her body, but she maintained control. "I'll say this only one more time, Mr. Aldrich. Your dog was poisoned."

"Probably got into some of the pesticides we use around the ranch,'' he said, running a hand through his dark hair.

''Did your wife tell you it was strychnine?''

''Yeah, well, they put that stuff in rat poison. Lots of rats around the ranch.''

And I'm looking at the biggest rat of all! ''Yes, it's found in rat poison, and it should also be used with extreme caution. I've notified the ACRARQCO. You could be held responsible for endangering your dog.''

''The what?''

''The Animal Control Rights and Regulations Quality Central Organization.''

He rolled his eyes. ''And what the devil is that?''

''Just what I said it is. And believe me, you don't want to tangle with them. Now, I would suggest you go home, Mr. Aldrich. We'll let you know when Bart is ready to be released.''

Hesitation was quickly replacing determination, and he backed up two steps. ''Yeah, well, when do you think that will be?''

''Perhaps as soon as tomorrow. Your

wife was quite distressed. I would suggest you go home and take care of her, and leave Bart to us. Good night, Mr. Aldrich.''

She opened the door, waited until he had exited, and then closed it firmly behind him. But it wasn't until she heard his car pull away that she allowed herself the luxury of a smile. She had buffaloed him, pure and simple, and it was wonderful!

Ben scratched his head. ''The what?''

Jennifer giggled. ''The ACRAROQC . . . no, it was the ACRARQCO—the Animal Control Rights and Regulations Quality Central Organization. It came to me out of the blue, Ben, but I had to do *something*. He was going to take Bart, and I wouldn't have been able to stop him.''

It was very late, and they were sitting in the office at the clinic. Ben shuffled some papers around on his desk, and shook his head. ''I can't believe he bought it.''

''Maybe he didn't, but he wasn't about to take the chance either. We'll probably never know how Bart ingested the poison, but—''

"You didn't tell him his wife thought the poison was meant for her, did you?"

"Of course not. Why make her life more miserable than it already is?"

"Did she tell you her life was miserable?" Ben asked curiously.

"No, but she's married to Richard Aldrich, isn't she? Isn't that enough?"

Ben was shuffling papers again. "You're not thinking about going to the sheriff with this, are you?"

"No, I'm not, because I haven't any proof. But I'm not going to let it go either. I plan to do a little digging, and a lot of watching."

"Whoa, Jennifer. Stop right there. You're a veterinarian, not a private detective."

Jennifer gave him a fetching grin. "Didn't I tell you I love to read mysteries? When I was little, it was Nancy Drew and the Hardy Boys. Sometimes, I created my own mysteries. Mrs. Deadson is a good example."

"Mrs. Deadson—Eva Deadson, who lived on River Road?"

"Right. I suppose it was the name that

triggered my childhood imagination, but I just *knew* she had dead bodies buried in her basement. It was a spooky old house to begin with, and she looked like my idea of a witch. Black hair, long nose, and all those blue veins on her thin hands. When she attended church on Sundays, I'd always manage to sit close. Well, not exactly *close,* but close enough to smell her sickly sweet perfume, and watch. She had a habit of tearing up wads of Kleenex all through the services, and then blowing her nose on her sleeve.''

Ben threw his head back and laughed. ''And that's what made you think she had dead bodies buried in her basement?''

''That and Mike Baker's observations. He lived down the road from her, and claimed her basement light was on all the time. One night he peeked in and saw her digging holes in the dirt floor. I didn't find out until after she died that she had been burying money. They found thousands of dollars. Apparently, she'd been burying her savings for years. When they dug it up, most of it had turned into confetti.''

''I remember that, and as I recall, you

and Mike Baker were quite a team before you went off to college. I remember seeing you together all the time. Two blond, blue-eyed, deeply tanned youngsters, who looked like they belonged to the sun.''

''And we're still friends. He's taken over the feed store for his father.''

''He's not married?''

''No, but he's been dating Sara Stevens, off and on.''

He shook his head. ''Wasn't she your best friend?''

''Still is. She's working at the doughnut shop and has put on twenty pounds. That's not meant to be a put-down. She was always painfully thin. Now she looks wonderful.''

Ben smacked his lips. ''I can understand putting on weight when you work in a doughnut shop. Raised doughnuts with gooey centers. All that fresh cake and sugar. If I'm within a block of the aroma, I lose control. Does it bother you that she's dating your old boyfriend?''

''No, it doesn't, because Mike and I were never in love. We were good friends—more like a sister and brother.''

Ben sighed. "You're a beautiful young woman. You should have a social life. Having a career is one thing, but . . ."

"I'm going to the Summer Swing dance with Willy Ashton on Saturday night. Does that make you feel better?"

"Willy Ashton—the lawyer?"

"Yes. We went to school together too, and we're still good friends." She shrugged into her sweater. "Don't forget to reschedule your doctor's appointment."

"First thing in the morning," he assured her.

"And I'll see you first thing in the morning, but if you need me—"

Ben raised a hand. "I'll call."

Jennifer left the clinic knowing he wouldn't call, not even if he had an emergency, because he wouldn't want to disturb her sleep. He was a caring man, and that was one of the reasons he was a good vet. She could only hope that someday, she would be half as worthy.

"You can't exist on five hours' sleep," Emma admonished Jennifer the next morning over breakfast. "And only toast and coffee? You're not going to gain weight that way!''

Wes placed his cereal bowl in the sink and chuckled. "She's been on the warpath all morning, Jennifer, but things really heated up when she heard you in the exercise room."

Emma's cheeks were pink from all her angry bustling around, and she fanned her face with her apron. "When you brought all that *stuff* home from Michigan, I gladly gave up my sewing room because I didn't want it all over the house. I gladly moved my things to the sun room, never dreaming you were going to turn my sewing room into a physical fitness center. It looks like those places you see on TV—a roomful of hard bodies, covered with sweat. Arnold Schwarzenegger bodies."

Jennifer made a muscle with her arm and giggled. "Don't worry, Emma. I'll never look like Arnie."

"Hmm. Well, in case you haven't noticed, your grandfather is wearing sweat clothes, and took a run to the river, even before the sun was up. Next, he'll be in *that* room, running on that *thing*, and pumping iron.''

''That *thing* is a treadmill, Emma.''

''Hamsters and mice use treadmills in their cages,'' Emma groused.

''Physical fitness is important,'' Jennifer reasoned. ''And age shouldn't be a factor. But it is important to check with a doctor before you begin any kind of exercise program.''

''I can take the hint,'' Wes said. ''But I'm way ahead of you. I made an appointment with the doc for tomorrow afternoon.''

''One of the new doctors over at the hospital?''

''No way. Doc Chambers has been our family doctor for years, and that's the way it stands.''

Jennifer had her mouth open to remind her grandfather that Alan Chambers was pushing eighty, but the phone rang, and he took the call. ''It's Ben,'' he said, handing her the receiver.

''Hi, Jennifer. My doctor's appointment is set for two this afternoon, so you don't have to come in until then,'' Ben said wearily.

Jennifer sighed. "You should go home and get some sleep."

"I caught a few winks on the couch in my office. By the way, I released the collie. Aldrich was on the doorstep bright and early. I thought about pulling that ACR-whatever on him again, but I knew I wouldn't get it right. Besides, the collie was doing so well, there really wasn't a good reason to keep him."

"Any calls on the ad?"

"One. Female. She's coming in tomorrow morning for an interview."

"Good! I'll see you this afternoon."

"Sounds like you have most of the day off," Wes said after Jennifer had hung up.

"I do, and I'm going to use it to check up on a patient. Remember I told you about the poisoned collie when I called yesterday afternoon? Well, Ben released him this morning, at the owner's insistence. The owner tried to get me to release him last night . . . " She took a deep breath. "I didn't mention the owner's name. It's Richard Aldrich."

Wes's eyes narrowed. "You're going out to the Aldrich ranch?"

"Is there a reason why I shouldn't?"

"No, of course not, but I can't help but remember the last time you were there, when Mary told you her husband didn't take kindly to company. I remember how upset you were. And, I must admit, that man is an enigma. He's alienated most of the folks in town, and he's all but kept the new wife a prisoner. She's only come into town a couple of times. Both times he was with her, and made her stay in the car. If you were to ask, most folks couldn't even tell you what she looks like."

"Red hair, blue eyes, petite. Very pretty."

Wes raised a brow. "You've seen her?"

"She's the one who brought the collie to the clinic. She was nearly hysterical, and I tried to calm her down." Jennifer was about to tell her grandfather the rest of it, but remembered, *Be sure your brain is engaged before your mouth is in motion.* It would serve no purpose to spread rumors like that when there wasn't any proof, and it could make things a whole lot worse. But there was one question she could ask, and she tried to make it sound casual.

"Remember that day I came across Mary on the riding trail, and you told me about Aldrich's other wives? Was that just a rumor? Or do you think it was the truth?"

"I would suspect it was the truth. He got drunk one night at Boodie's Roadhouse, and told everybody about his two pretty wives. That was shortly after he came to Calico, and long before he married Mary."

"Who told you?"

"Newt Jones. He was at the roadhouse that night for a pool tournament, and heard the whole thing. He also saw the way Aldrich was acting around the cocktail waitresses. He waylaid me on the street a few days later and told me I had to get Richard Aldrich into my fold, because the man was on a collision course with the devil. I told Newt that he would do better to worry about himself, that there was a pew in my church with his name on it, and God was waiting for *him.* That changed the course of the conversation, and he couldn't wait to get away from me. But I believed him. He was sober, and he was sober the night of the tournament. He might have had his problems, but he took the game of pool seriously, and was always sober when he played.''

''But didn't you think that was strange? I mean, for Richard Aldrich to behave that way? From everything I've heard, he has always been a recluse,'' Jennifer said.

''Not the first year. You were about ten at the time, and probably too young to remember, but he did a lot of socializing. The folks tried warming up to him, wanting him to feel at home, but it wasn't easy. He had a way about him that set everybody's teeth on edge.''

''Then maybe the town was responsible for turning him into a recluse.''

''Maybe, but I'm more inclined to believe his womanizing ways put him under. I think he was looking for a new wife. He courted a lot of available women—made each and every one of them think they were special, and then they found out he was courting all of them at the same time. He'd have four different dates in one night. When they realized what he was doing, the doors literally closed in his face. And that, my dear, is why I think he had to go out of the area to find his wife.''

"Mary, from Bismark, North Dakota."

"That's right. And now he's married to a woman from back East. But I'll tell you something, sweetheart. I've never stopped praying that someday he'll walk into my church, and want to call it home."

"And Newt Jones. Is he still around?"

"Sure he is. He's one of the old-timers who's putting up the senior citizens' center. At least it's keeping *him* out of trouble."

Jennifer's thoughts were on overload again, as she planned out her day. She had every intention of visiting the Aldrich ranch, but not until she made a few important stops along the way, and asked a few dozen questions. She was determined to get to the bottom of the mystery of the poisoned collie.

Chapter Three

Elmer Dodd had "coughed up the land for the senior citizens' center," as her grandfather had put it, and Jennifer could easily see why he also thought the land "wasn't fit to raise scrawny chickens." It was situated near the refuse disposal site south of town, and there wasn't a tree on the property. After she'd parked the Cherokee and the dust had settled, she also realized that the senior citizens who were building the two-story structure were working under deplorable conditions. There was only one portable toilet, no running water, and the weather forecaster had predicted it would reach ninety degrees by midday. She supposed the excitement of actually having a center they could call their own was what kept them going, and she could appreciate that, but many of these people were the actual founders of the town of Calico, and it didn't seem fair. Not when there were so many parks around. Any one of them could have been the site of the center, where the senior citizens would have had green grass and trees, and the beauty they richly deserved.

She found an elderly lady under a canvas awning—the only shade anywhere—pouring lemonade into paper cups, and asked, "Who's in charge?"

The woman looked surprised, and cupped a hand around her ear. "What was that?"

Jennifer raised her voice. "Who is in charge?"

"Why, Digger Meehan. That's him over there in the hard hat."

Jennifer smoothed down her flowered sundress, wishing she had worn jeans and running shoes, and made her way over mounds of dirt and around piles of lumber.

By the time she reached the burly foreman, who was yelling at a skinny little
man because he had cut a board the wrong
length, her sandals were filled with dirt,
and perspiration drenched her clothing.
When he was through with his tirade, she
demanded, ''Who put you in charge?''

He looked at her as though she had just
flown in from Mars and snapped, ''Who
the heck are you?''

''I'm a concerned citizen. I'm also a
member of the SCRC, and I just might
have to shut this operation down.''

''Say what?''

If it had worked for Richard Aldrich,
maybe it would work for this man. She
squared her shoulders. ''The Senior Citizens' Rights Commission. Now, I'll ask
you again. Who put you in charge?''

''Elmer Dodd. It's his property. You
have a bone to pick, pick it with him.''

''And your name is?''

''Digger Meehan.''

''Are you from around here?''

''North Platte. I go where the work
is.''

Jennifer wished she had a notebook so

she would look more official, but at least she was storing all the information in her head. "Who supplied the building material?"

"Dodd. Why?"

She motioned toward a box of nails. "Used nails, and most of them are bent, and the wood is full of knotholes. I doubt that this structure will pass inspection when it's completed."

"It'll pass. Now, if you don't mind, I've got work to do."

"I'd like to talk to Newt Jones."

"What's he done?" the man asked.

Jennifer raised her chin. "My business is with him."

"He's working on the second floor, but you can't go in there without a hard hat."

"Then give me a hard hat."

He smirked. "Don't have a spare one available."

"Then I would suggest you give me yours."

"Listen, Lady . . ."

"It's either that, or I go make a few phone calls."

The look of uncertainty on his face was

quite remarkable, as he pulled off his hat. "It ain't gonna fit," he muttered.

Jennifer snapped her fingers, the gesture of a brilliant thought, and gave him an equally brilliant smile. "Then I would suggest you go get Mr. Jones. I'll talk to him out here."

Uncertainty again, but he walked into the building.

A few minutes later, a tall, thin man ambled out, carrying his hard hat. He had big ears, a bald head, and a frown between his eyes. "You want to see me?"

"I do. Let's go get a glass of lemonade."

"It ain't my break."

"It is now."

A few minutes later, they stood under the awning sipping lemonade, and Jennifer lowered her voice. "I would appreciate it if you would keep this conversation to yourself. Deal?"

Newt Jones shrugged. "It depends."

"My name is Jennifer Gray—"

He looked surprised. "The pastor's kid?"

"I'm his granddaughter. My grandfather

told me he had a conversation with you a long, long time ago, regarding Richard Aldrich.''

He wiped his forehead with a soiled handkerchief. ''How long ago?''

''Maybe fourteen years or so.''

He gave a healthy snort. ''And you expect me to remember back that far? Lady, sometimes I can't remember what day it is.''

''Well, would you try to remember? It's really important. You were in Boodie's Roadhouse, getting ready for a pool tournament. Richard Aldrich was there, talking about his two pretty wives. He was also making passes at the cocktail waitresses, and you were angry.''

Newt looked up at the sky. ''Yeah, I was mad. Nobody was interested in the tournament. All eyes were on Aldrich.''

''That's right, and a few days later, you talked to my grandfather.''

''Yeah. I told him Aldrich was on his way to see the devil.''

Jennifer took a deep breath. ''If you can, I'd like you to go back to that night at the roadhouse, Mr. Jones. I'd like you to try to remember what the man said. Specifically, did he mention his wives' names?''

Newt closed one eye, like he was sizing her up. ''What do you want to know for?''

''I'm a veterinarian, and Mr. Aldrich's dog is one of my patients.''

''So?''

''I'm not at liberty to discuss it, Mr. Jones, but like I said, it *is* important.''

''Yeah, well, I guess he mentioned a name. Said it was his first wife. Said she was the sweetest of all. 'Course, that was before he moved to Calico. Said her name was Audra, or Audrey, or something like that. No, it was Addy. Yeah, Addy. Addy Allison from Sioux Falls. I guess I remember because I had a cousin named Addy.''

''Can you remember anything else about that evening?''

''Other than the fact that he screwed up the tournament? Not really . . . Wait a minute. He bought drinks for everybody, and said he was celebrating. Didn't say why, and nobody asked.''

''And?''

"And that's it."

Jennifer leaned over and kissed his cheek. "Thanks, Mr. Jones. You're a sweetheart, and you really have a very good memory."

"Can I go back to work now?"

"Sure, but I have to ask you. Do you enjoy working here?"

"Heck, no, but I can see what we'll have at the end. That makes it worth it."

But did it? Jennifer wondered as she made her way to the Cherokee. And what would they have at the end, *if* the building managed to pass inspection? It would be a place where they could meet and share their memories. But when they looked out the windows, they wouldn't see the town that had created those memories. They would see the refuse disposal site, and a desolate wasteland.

"Uh-oh. I can tell by the look on your face something's up. Don't tell me you've changed your mind about going to the dance Saturday night."

Willy Ashton's tiny, cluttered office was on the first floor of the only professional building in town, and faced the courthouse. It was convenient for Willy because he spent so much time in court, but the massive domed building also obstructed the breeze coming off the river. At the moment, the office was stifling.

Jennifer fanned her face with a manila folder, and accepted a glass of ice water. "No, I haven't changed my mind, and I'm looking forward to the dance."

"Well, something's on your mind."

Willy had clear blue eyes, a head of dark brown, curly hair, and one of those wonderfully open faces that brought on a smile even when you were feeling down. The teachers had adored him in school, and all the kids had wanted to be his pal. It was a good quality to have when you were a defense attorney.

"I have a lot on my mind, Willy. I was afraid you might be in court."

"Not until one o'clock, so I'm all yours."

He winked at her, and she smiled. "How much do you know about Richard Aldrich?"

"Not much. Nobody does. Nobody

cares. He's not exactly Calico's most beloved citizen. Have you had a run-in with him?''

"Sort of. His dog was poisoned, and his wife brought the dog to the clinic. I stayed at the clinic last night to watch the dog, and a cat recovering from surgery, and around ten o'clock Aldrich arrived and demanded I release the dog. That's an abbreviated version, Willy, and there is a bottom line. The wife thinks the poison was meant for her. She said she was making a hamburger patty, the dog ate the patty, and then he began acting strange. He had all the classic symptoms of strychnine poisoning. They live on a ranch, so it isn't unusual to have rat poison around, and I tried to explain that it was possible the dog could have gotten into rat poison before he ate the patty. But I also told her if she was convinced the poison was in the hamburger, she should call the authorities, and have the hamburger analyzed. At that point, she retracted everything she'd said. She asked *me* to forget what she'd said, and became even more distraught. It left me with one thought—whether the hamburger was poisoned or not, *she* thought it was.''

''Did you report it to the sheriff?'' Willy asked thoughtfully.

''No, because she said she was mistaken. She also said she threw the hamburger away. But I was left with a feeling, and I haven't been able to shake it. I can't explain it, Willy, but I'd like to do a little checking. Quietly and discreetly. And I need your help. Nobody knows about this except you and Ben, and that's the way I'd like to keep it.''

Willy sucked in his cheeks, and pursed his lips. ''That's pretty heavy stuff, Jennifer, and maybe you'd better think it out before you go nosing around. If Richard Aldrich decided to kill his wife, why would he put strychnine in the hamburger? Sounds pretty dumb to me. That would make him the prime suspect.''

''I know, but . . .'' She placed the folder on the desk, and walked to the window. ''Aldrich has been married four times, but his present wife, Pam, only knows about Mary, who died the year I went away to college. He married the other two before he moved to Calico.''

''Maybe he didn't tell her about the first two because he didn't want to dredge up the past.''

''That's what Ben said.''

''I take it your grandfather doesn't know about this?''

''Not about the alleged tainted hamburger. I didn't want to worry him, or have him think I was getting in over my head.''

''Well, aren't you?''

''Maybe, but it's my nature to be curious. I also find it curious, for a man who has had so many wives, to go nearly six years without a wife. He was married to Mary for a year before she died, and he's been married to Pam for nearly a year. That puts nearly six years in between.''

Willy joined Jennifer at the window, and put an arm around her shoulder. ''Are you suggesting Aldrich killed all his wives?''

''Hmm, and you're a mind reader, too. He kept Mary a virtual prisoner, and he's doing the same thing to Pam. Why? I also want to know what Mary died of, and I want to locate his other wives, *if* they are

alive. I already have the name of his first
wife—Addy Allison, from Sioux Falls.''

"I'm impressed. How did you manage
that?''

Jennifer told him, which also renewed
her anger. ''By the way, are you aware of
what's going on over there?''

"You mean at the senior citizens' center? Last I heard, they have the framework
up.''

"Yeah, and their working conditions are
deplorable. And if that isn't bad enough,
it's practically on top of the refuse disposal site, and there isn't a tree on the
property. So Elmer Dodd is the *big man*
because he's given them the land and do-
nated the building material. Inferior building material, I might add, hardly fit to
build a chicken coop. Why couldn't the
town donate one of the parks for the pro-
ject? And the lumber, for that matter?
Why do the old-timers have to settle for
crumbs, when most of them built this
town? It makes me so angry, I could chew
those old rusty bent nails they're using!
Oh, I know—Grandfather told me a couple of the parks are going to be turned into

commercial property. Big deal. And that's another thing. . . . ''

Willy's chuckle was warm. "You haven't changed, Jenny. You were a crusader in school too."

"Nobody has called me Jenny in years. It makes me feel as though I still have braces on my teeth."

"Heaven forbid," he said, with a twinkle in his eye.

"Laugh if you want, but you had better believe I'm going to do some screaming."

"Scream loud enough, and maybe it'll take your mind off Aldrich and his wives, alive *and* dead."

"Never! Are you going to help me, or not?"

He smoothed back a blond tendril from her forehead, and nodded. "Sure, I'll help. I like a good mystery as well as the next guy, but I think we had better tread with the utmost care."

"Utmost care," she promised, giving him a hug. "First of all, I'd like a copy of Mary's death certificate."

"Was Doc Chambers the attending physician?"

"I doubt it. Aldrich had already alienated most of the town by that time, so they
probably went to a doctor in North Platte,
if Mary had a doctor. That's just a guess,
of course."

"Was she buried in the town cemetery?"

"I have no idea."

"Okay, I'll add it to the list of things to
check out. What else?"

"We have to find somebody we can trust
to do some digging. Both in Bismarck and
Sioux Falls."

"Bismarck?"

"Mary was supposedly from Bismarck.
I'd go myself, but I can't leave Ben. Nor
would I want to throw Grandfather into a
tizzy."

"I have a cousin who lives near Bismarck, and I know a private detective in
Sioux Falls. We went to college together.
He was two years ahead of me, but we
were good friends."

"Like us, huh?" Jennifer said, giving
him a luminous smile. "Did I pick the
right guy, or what? Tell your cousin and

your PI friend I'll pay them to snoop around.''

''I guarantee they won't take your money, Jennifer, but I'll make the offer. What do you want them to do?''

''Basically the same thing, only they'll be working with different time periods. Your cousin will have to go back about seven years to find the marriage license.''

''*If* they were married in Bismarck.''

''If they weren't, it's a dead end, because I don't know Mary's maiden name. But if they were, then he'll have her maiden name, and if he can locate her family, it would sure help. Have him get me a phone number, and I'll take it from there. Same with your friend in Sioux Falls, but he'll have to go back over fifteen years. Maybe even sixteen or seventeen.

''Also, and I don't know how difficult it's going to be, I'd like to know who sold Aldrich the ranch, and who holds the mortgage. I know after Mr. Treemont died, it was vacant a long time before Aldrich bought it. He had to sign loan papers, Willy, and that would give us some background on the man.''

"We have one bank in town, and one realtor," Willy reasoned. "So it shouldn't be difficult."

"I've also heard he has sold off most of his cattle. That sounds like he's having financial difficulties. I'm having a hard time with that too, because he had a tremendous herd two years ago. When I came home on vacation that summer, he was the talk of the town. Five thousand head of cattle, approximately a thousand pounds each. Ninety cents to a dollar a pound on the hoof. It doesn't take a mathematical genius to figure out that amounts a lot of money. I also heard he was getting tremendous stud fees for three prize bulls. People were bringing him their heifers from all over the state. And now he's broke? He also has a ranch hand I'd like to do some checking on, but I'll take care of that myself.'"

"What's with the ranch hand?"

"Aldrich claims the man is a vet, but I have my doubts."

"It's not unusual for a large cattle ranch to have their own veterinarian."

"I know, but this one doesn't ring true.

But that's another story, and now I've got
to go.''

''Back to work?''

''No. I'm going to go out to the Aldrich
ranch and check on the dog.''

Willy grinned. ''Among other things?''

''Among other things. Thanks, Willy. I
owe you one.''

''No, you don't. Just go the dance with
me Saturday night, and we'll call it even.''

It was close to lunchtime when Jennifer
pulled up in the graveled parking area of
Aldrich's ranch. Everything looked the
same as she remembered it, only now it
was unkempt. The house badly needed a
coat of paint, and the lawn area needed to
be mowed. Where she remembered having
seen a colorful display of purple asters, lo-
belia, and crimson-colored roses, unsightly
weeds now stood two feet high. Even the
peachleaf willow drooped in discontent-
ment. Was the fact that Aldrich was finan-
cially distressed the answer? Or was it
simply neglect? She walked up to the porch
and knocked, going over her story in the
event Richard Aldrich opened the door.

But it was Pam Aldrich who opened the door a crack, and the surprise on her face was obvious. She had also been crying. "Y-you shouldn't be here," she stammered.

"I'd like to see Bart," Jennifer said, using her most professional tone.

"I don't think—"

"Who is it?" Richard Aldrich said, suddenly appearing over his wife's shoulder.

Jennifer gave him her brightest smile. "Hello, Mr. Aldrich. I'd like to check on Bart."

His face was as dark as a thundercloud. "Sorry, but that won't be possible. The dog died a couple of hours ago."

Stunned by the news and by the callousness in his voice, Jennifer demanded, "How did it happen?"

"He was poisoned, remember?"

"Yes, and he was also on the mend. Ben Copeland would never have allowed you to take him home if he wasn't."

"Yeah, well, that just shows you what kind of an incompetent hick-town vet he is."

Aldrich started to close the door, but

Jennifer put her foot in the doorway. "What did you do with the body?"

"Buried it so it wouldn't attract coyotes."

Jennifer looked at Pam, and gave her a gentle smile. "If you want to talk about this, I'll be at the clinic later this afternoon."

This time, Jennifer couldn't prevent the door from closing firmly in her face.

Fuming and heartsick, she headed for the Jeep, and was about to open the door when movement caught her eye. Vultures were circling near a small ridge east of the property. It wasn't unusual to see the scavengers, she reminded herself as she pulled out on the dirt road, and yet . . . She shook her head and gripped the wheel, aware that her hyperactive imagination was in overdrive again. But what if . . .

Jennifer looked back. When she could no longer see the ranch house, she pulled over under a stand of trees and took a deep breath. There were no fences here, only open grassland, and so the choice was hers. She could either hike to the ridge, or attempt to drive across the sandy loam that was so prevalent in the area. Reminding herself she had a four-wheel-drive vehicle, she looked at her watch, and the decision was made.

Ten minutes later, Jennifer found the dog's body. It had been unceremoniously dumped in a small gully, and even before she examined it, she knew what she would find. The dog had been shot through the head.

Chapter Four

Ben was unlocking the back door to the clinic when Jennifer pulled up. She saw the expression of disbelief on his face when she climbed out of the Jeep, and she could hardly have expected less. She knew what she looked like. Her dress was in tatters, and perspiration had mingled with the dirt on her skin, creating a muddy mess.

"Don't say it," she muttered. "Just help me with Bart."

"Bart? What do you mean, Jennifer? What's happened?"

"Somebody shot him," she said, walking to the back of the vehicle. Tears filled her eyes. "Shot him through the head, and dumped his body in a gully. Well, I wasn't about to leave him there. First of all, I want the bullet, and then I want to bury him in the pet cemetery. He deserves that much, at least."

Ben looked at the dog and shuddered. "Maybe you'd better start from the beginning."

"Let's get him into the clinic first . . . No, on second thought, maybe you'd better tell me what the doctor said. If you're not able to lift him—"

"It's an ulcer, Jennifer, and that doesn't put me on my deathbed. Some medicine and the proper diet, and I'll live long enough to enjoy my retirement."

"But ulcers can be serious. . . . "

"And they can heal up too. Let's get this over with."

After they had the dog on an examining table in the emergency room, Jennifer washed her hands and face, but she couldn't wash away the tears. "When I arrived at the ranch, Pam opened the door. She'd been crying, and then Aldrich . . . well, let's just say he was looming over his wife's shoulder, and couldn't wait to tell me the dog was dead,'' she explained.

Ben was gathering the necessary surgical instruments and asked, ''He admitted to shooting the dog?''

''No, he said the dog died, and that he'd buried the body—didn't want to attract coyotes. And then he closed the door in my face. I was furious, of course, and sick. I drove away, and that's when I saw the vultures. . . . Don't ask me how I knew it was Bart. It was a struggle to get him up to the Jeep, but I wasn't going to give up.''

Ben ran a hand over the dog's limp coat, and gritted his teeth. ''There has to be a place in hell for a man like that.''

''That's right, and if he can kill his dog, who knows what else he is capable of? I'll never forget the look on Pam's face, or the fear in her eyes. She's in danger, Ben. I believe that with all my heart.''

Ben was examining the wound. ''So how do we prove it?''

''I've already got the wheels in motion. I don't want to go into details, because the less you know, the better. But keep your fingers crossed. Maybe we'll get lucky.''

Twenty minutes later, Ben had the bullet in a metal tray, and the body wrapped in plastic. Jennifer had called the pet cemetery, and somebody was coming to pick up the remains.

Ben studied the bullet and shook his head. ''And I suppose you're going to pay for the burial?''

''Of course I am, even though I'd love to send the bill to Aldrich.''

''And if he happens to ride out to the gully and can't find the body?''

Jennifer shrugged. ''He'll probably think a coyote carted it off. Though to tell you the truth, I don't care what he thinks. The gloves are off, Ben. I'm going to take the bullet to Sheriff Cody, and tell him everything, and where I found the body. If that points the finger at Aldrich, so be it.''

''You're going to tell him *everything?*''

''Well, not everything. I haven't got the kind of proof to tell him Aldrich is trying to kill his wife, but I'll give him enough to make him want to take some action. The people in Calico don't go around shooting their animals, Ben. And that maniac isn't going to get away with it!''

Ben reached in his pocket and pulled out three twenties. ''Add this to the pot, Jennifer. You shouldn't have to pay for the burial alone.''

''Thanks,'' she said, feeling the sting of tears behind her eyes again.

The bells on the front door tinkled, and Jennifer sighed. ''It's too soon for the pickup from the cemetery, and they'll probably come in the back way. So it must be a patient.''

''You get it,'' Ben said. ''I'll stay with the dog.''

She gave him a grateful smile, because the lump wrapped in plastic was making her physically ill. Bart had been a beautiful, trusting animal, and now this . . .

Forgetting what she looked like for a moment, until she saw the look on the girl's face, Jennifer tried for a lame excuse. ''It's been a busy day,'' she said sheepishly to the girl at the door.

The girl grinned. ''Looks like you wrestled with a bull, and the bull won. My name is Tina Allen. I called about the ad in the paper. I know my interview isn't until to-morrow morning, but I just couldn't wait that long.''

Jennifer shook the girl's hand, and took inventory. Warm brown hair, clear brown eyes and a turned-up nose. She was cute and eager, and Jennifer liked her immedi-ately. ''I'm Jennifer Gray, Dr. Copeland's assistant. I'm afraid this isn't the best time, but on the other hand, if you're going to work for a veterinarian, you might as well learn right now that things can get pretty rough. We have a dead collie in the back, and we're waiting for somebody from the pet cemetery to pick him up. Now, if you'd like to come back tomorrow . . .''

Tears filled Tina Allen's eyes, but her jaw was firm. ''I had a dog when I was a little kid. Part collie and part Lab. He got hit by a car in front of our house. I sat right there in the middle of the road, holding him in my arms, and begging the onlookers to do something. He was already dead, of course, but I didn't know that. I kept think-ing if I knew what to do, I could save him. That's the day I decided I wanted to be a vet.''

Jennifer took a deep, cleansing breath. ''Then working here would mean more to you than just a job.''

''Much, much more. I have two years left of high school, and then I'm going to college. If I keep my grades up, maybe I'll get accepted into veterinary school, and that's my dream.''

Jennifer felt the girl's grief, right to her core, but she also felt her determination, because it was so much like her own. ''This collie wasn't hit by a car, Tina. Somebody shot him in the head . . .''

Tina's face turned pale, and she swayed slightly. Then heartfelt anger took over. ''That's awful. Who would do such a terrible thing?''

''A crazy person who doesn't have the right to be called a human being.''

A few minutes later, Ben walked into the waiting room, and managed a smile. ''What can we do for you, young lady?''

Jennifer spoke up. ''This is Dr. Copeland, Tina, but you had better call him Ben. Ben, this is Tina Allen, the young lady who answered the ad. She didn't want to wait until tomorrow. I told her about the collie.''

Ben grimaced. "We do our best to save lives, Tina. We're not always successful, of course, but something like this . . . It's a heartbreaker. Such a darn shame."

"Why don't you take Tina into your office and give her a soda, Ben? You can get acquainted while I wait for the pickup."

Ben smiled at Tina, and it was a smile that warmed Jennifer's heart. He liked her too.

By five o'clock, Tina had filled out the necessary paperwork, and they had given her a tour of the facility. Next came the interview. And every question was answered with the sincerity of someone who was on the brink of a career in veterinary medicine.

Finally, it was time to lock up and call it a day.

Tina was on her way out the door, but stopped for one last question. "I know that unless you have a patient that needs constant care, the animals are left alone at night. But don't they get lonely? I mean, they're away from their owners, and . . ."

Jennifer smiled. "I know how you feel.

I felt the same way, but the animals really do adapt well, and we never have much more than an occasional overnighter, unless surgery is involved, or some serious injury or illness. Then, of course, we work around the clock.''

"Well, if you ever need a baby-sitter, I'm available.''

Jennifer watched Tina ride away on her bicycle, and felt a lump form in her throat. "She reminds me of me when I was that age," she said a bit wistfully.

Ben gave Jennifer a hug. "I was thinking the same thing.''

It was too late to talk to the sheriff, so Jennifer went home, with the bullet in her purse, and prayed her grandfather and Emma were busy so she could sneak off to her room without getting the third degree. Unfortunately, they were sitting on the front porch, drinking iced tea.

Emma spoke first, and her voice actually quavered. "Tell us you weren't in an accident, and then I'll tell my heart to start beating.''

Jennifer tried her lame excuse again. "It's been a busy day."

Wes made a clicking sound with his tongue. "Busy doing what? Fighting off a band of modern-day cattle rustlers? You look like you've been through a war."

"You're not far wrong. I'll go freshen up, and then I'll tell you all about it."

She made a hasty retreat, but not before Emma said, "You'd better do a lot more than 'freshen up,' young lady."

Jennifer hurried upstairs, breathing in deeply of the wonderful aromas coming from the kitchen. She sorted through what she could tell Wes and Emma. Actually, it was a matter of how *much* she should tell them, and she truly hated all this secrecy. They'd always had an open, honest relationship, yet she didn't want to worry them.

It wasn't until after she'd taken a shower and slipped into shorts and a blouse, that she realized the truth. The *real* truth. It wasn't so much a matter of worrying them; she didn't want to get reprimanded for poking her nose into a situation where it didn't belong.

She was still debating the issue when she

joined them in the kitchen and, as usual, her grandfather knew her too well.

He handed her a glass of iced tea and said, "Okay, out with it, young lady. You've been pussyfooting around since yesterday, and I think it's time you told us the truth. Does this have anything to do with Richard Aldrich and the poisoned dog?"

Jennifer sat down at the kitchen table and felt her shoulders slump. "It has everything to do with it."

By the time Jennifer started at the beginning and had gone through the whole incredible story, dinner was on the table. But nobody was hungry.

Wes picked at the slices of pot roast on his plate, and shook his head. "And you plan on talking to the sheriff tomorrow?"

"First thing in the morning. Willy didn't call, did he?"

"No, but I would think a background investigation like that would take some time. You did get one call, from Amy Thompson. She said to tell you the wedding invitations went out long before you returned to Calico, but you're invited. I don't suppose it's possible now for you to attend, is it?''

''No, it isn't. Saturday is usually a big day at the clinic, and with Tina in training, and the dance Saturday night . . . I'll get them a nice gift, though, and take Amy to lunch after they get back from their honeymoon. They *are* going on a honeymoon, aren't they?''

''Disney World in Florida, if you can believe it. The groom's parents have money, and the kids had the whole world to choose from.''

Jennifer grinned. ''Disney World is a world in itself, Grandfather. They'll have a wonderful time.''

''Hmm. So this Tina Allen is new in town?''

''Well, not *new* new. They've been here about six months. Her father is a doctor at the new hospital—internal medicine.''

Emma, who had been quiet through most of the conversation, spoke up. ''*Murder She Wrote.* I saw the show last season. A man was killing his wife with small amounts of arsenic. Jessica Fletcher solved the case, of course, but it wasn't easy. Are you sure the dog ingested strychnine?''

Jennifer nearly choked on a bit of broccoli. For one thing, this wasn't the way this was supposed to be going. She was supposed to be getting a dressing-down for acting like a one-man band, and here they were going along with her. ''The symptoms were classic, Emma.''

''Can you kill somebody with strychnine, a little bit at a time?'' Emma asked thoughtfully.

''I don't think so. It would take a large dose of strychnine at one time to do the job.''

''So maybe the dog ingested rat poison, and Aldrich is trying to kill his wife with arsenic. And maybe he shot the dog out of pure orneriness. He doesn't sound like a very nice man.''

''And may God have mercy on his soul,'' Wes said, shaking his head in disbelief.

Jennifer sighed. ''I know you try to find the good in everybody, Grandfather, but sometimes you can't. The man is evil, and I think his wife is in danger.''

"Potatoes," Emma said, placing a generous portion of mashed potatoes on Jennifer's plate. "That should put the weight on, and give you some energy. I also bought you some vitamins. One before bedtime every night. You hear?"

"I hear," Jennifer said, unable to hold back the smile. She was surrounded by love and understanding, and it felt wonderful.

Wes helped himself to a dollop of mashed potatoes too, and said, "So what did you think of the senior citizens' center?"

Jennifer rolled her eyes. "I wasn't impressed, and I'm going to complain to Elmer Dodd the first chance I get. The working conditions are terrible, and you're quite right that the land isn't fit for raising scrawny chickens. To add insult to injury, Dodd has given them inferior building supplies. The foreman says it will pass inspection when the time comes, but I have my doubts."

Wes and Emma exchanged glances, and Wes smiled. "Uh-huh. I knew that's the attitude you'd probably take. Welcome home, sweetheart. We live in a town called

Calico, but it could easily be renamed Disharmony. Unfortunately, I don't think we can do much about it.''

"We? What's this 'we' stuff? You have a mouse in your pocket?''

Wes flushed rosy pink, and Jennifer giggled, remembering the old cliché from years ago. She would say ''we'' this or ''we'' that, and he'd always say, ''You have a mouse in your pocket?'' And yet he had always been there for her, offering to help her in any way he could. She had the feeling it wouldn't be any different this time, and she loved him with all her heart.

Jennifer was on the porch later that night for one last breath of fresh air before turning in, when her grandfather joined her. Nothing had changed here, even though the white wicker furniture had been given a new coat of paint. The porch swing with its brightly flowered pillows still squeaked, reminding her of all the nights she had sat beside her grandfather, pouring out her dreams. And oh, the sweet scent of honeysuckle! It had been growing over the trellis at the end of the porch for as long as she could remember. She rested her head against Wes's shoulder, watched the fireflies dance in the moonlight, and breathed in deeply.

Wes gave her a hug and said, "I know you don't want to hear an old man's advice, but I'm going to give it to you anyway. Be careful, sweetheart. Richard Aldrich could be a dangerous man."

Another sigh. "I know, and that's why it's so important to see this through. Calico might be going through a lot of changes and growing pains, Grandfather, but there is no room for someone as nasty as Aldrich. None of us will be safe until that man is apprehended."

"Sounds like a monumental task to me."

"Maybe, but way back when, you told me there was no mountain that was too high to climb. I believed that then, and I believe that now. But I could use some help."

"A few prayers?"

"A lot of prayers. And a lot of luck."

Jennifer was in the sheriff's office the following morning before Nettie, the clerk, had plugged in the coffeepot.

Sheriff Cody gave Jennifer a hearty embrace, and beamed. ''I heard you were back. Working for old Ben Copeland, are you?''

''Yes, but he isn't *that* old.'' She plunked the bullet on his desk. ''I need the caliber.''

He raised a brow, and Nettie looked over his shoulder. ''It's a thirty-thirty,'' she said, giving Jennifer a wink.

Nettie Balkin, who was the clerk, secretary and dispatcher, had been around forever. Almost as long as Jim Cody, and they looked enough alike to be brother and sister. Both were pleasingly plump with gray hair and genuine wide smiles. The sheriff's department, covering all of Peace County, consisted of the sheriff, eight deputies and four patrol cars. And not to be overlooked was Mayor Attwater, who liked to think he ran the sheriff's department, but didn't. Sheriff Cody had been elected by the county over and over again because of his expertise and his sense of fairness, and that's what Jennifer was counting on now.

"Deer rifle?" she speculated.

Sheriff Cody nodded. "More than likely a Winchester. What's this all about, Jennifer?"

She sat down in the chair beside the sheriff's desk, and got right to it. "Somebody shot Richard Aldrich's collie about a quarter mile from his ranch. I found the body. Ben recovered the bullet. I just thought you should know some idiot is out there killing animals."

"A quarter of a mile from the ranch? Was the dog on his property?"

"I don't know, but it wasn't fenced. I saw vultures swooping, and found the dog in a gully."

The sheriff drummed his fingers on his desk. "And why were you out at the Aldrich ranch?"

"The day before, Aldrich's wife brought the dog into the clinic. He was suffering from strychnine poisoning, and we almost lost him."

"Rat poison?"

"Maybe. We wanted to keep him a few

days for observation, but the husband insisted on taking him home the next morning.''

''When was this?''

''Yesterday morning. Around noon, I went out to the ranch to check up on him, and was told the dog was dead. I was also told the dog had been buried.''

''Aldrich told you?''

''Yes. I also got the door slammed in my face. On my way out, I saw the circling vultures, and had a hunch. Somebody shot the dog in the head.''

Nettie cursed under her breath, and the sheriff shook his head. ''I'm afraid we can't do much about something like this, Jennifer. First of all, we have no way of knowing who actually killed the dog.''

''Can't you match the bullet to the gun?''

''Sure, if we could get our hands on the gun. You think he's gonna turn over all the weapons he has on the ranch? And we sure can't go in with a search warrant. We'd need probable cause for that. I hate to say it, but it's only a dog. Normal rules and penal codes don't apply.''

''What about cruelty to animals?''

''Got to prove that too, little lady. Hey, I don't like the man. Most of the folks in town feel the same way, and nobody wants to see an animal maimed or killed. But my hands are tied.''

Jennifer took the cup of coffee Nettie handed her, and knew she had to make a decision. So what if it backfired? It was all speculation anyway. ''What would you say if I said I think Richard Aldrich is going to kill his wife?''

The sheriff jerked in amazement and accidentally slopped coffee on his desk. ''I'd say that's a pretty serious accusation.''

''I'm not making an accusation. I'm simply stating what I think. I think he killed Mary too, and maybe his other wives.''

''Mary—he married her about six or seven years ago. Everybody thought she was touched in the head.''

''Yes, but I didn't. That was the same year I went off to college. I came home for Christmas vacation, and found out she'd passed away.''

''Yeah, well, you're right that sure was quick. One minute she was alive, the next minute she was dead. He shipped the body to her parents, as I recall. He was married before?''

''Yes, two times. Mary was number three, Pam is number four. Do you know if Dr. Chambers was Mary's attending physician? Or if he signed the death certificate?''

''I know for a fact he didn't. They had a doctor from out of the area.''

''Hmm. Well, I guess that's about it. Say hello to your wife.''

''Oh, no you don't! You're not gonna walk out of here and leave it like that. Come clean, Jennifer. There has to be more to this.''

''Actually, there isn't, Sheriff. It's just a gut feeling. I think the man is despicable, but that doesn't make him a killer. And I know you can't help Pam unless she wants your help.''

''Pam, the wife?''

''Yes, and I'm seeing the same fear in her eyes I saw in Mary's eyes that summer before she died.''

''And?''

Jennifer swung her leg back and forth.

"And Pam said the strychnine was in the hamburger, and was meant for her."

"Whoa! Why didn't you tell me that before?"

"Because she took it all back after I said if she thought somebody was trying to kill her, she should get in touch with the authorities. She said she couldn't do that. She'd gotten rid of the hamburger, for one thing. She said Bart, the dog, probably ate a dead rat that had been poisoned with strychnine. That was after I put the idea in her head, of course, and . . ."

The sheriff ran a hand through his thinning hair. "Did you go away to veterinary school or to Quantico?"

"Quantico?"

"Yeah, where they train all good FBI agents."

Jennifer smiled. "I'll take that as a compliment. I went to vet school, Sheriff Cody, and I love animals. And I care about people. This has really got me riled up."

"I can tell. Well, I guess I can go talk to the man about the dog, at least. Stir him up a little. Over the years, I've learned to sort out truth and lies. If he's lying, I'll know it. Can't say how I'll handle it if he is, but what the hey? It's about time I had to use my head for something besides a hat rack.''

''You're not going to tell him I found the dog, are you?''

''No way. I'll talk to him about the poisoning, and the fact that the dog died.''

Jennifer finished her coffee, tossed the Styrofoam cup in the wastebasket, and got to her feet. ''You might want to tell him the ACRARQCO sent you out to ask some questions.''

''The what?''

''The Animal Control Rights and Regulations Quality Central Organization. There isn't any such organization, of course, but I had to think of something to stop him from taking the collie home too soon. That was the first night. Ben released the dog the next day because he was so much better. Anyway, I told Aldrich the ACRARQCO was probably going to investigate him for leaving poison around where his dog could get into it.''

Nettie muttered, ''Sounds to me as

though there *should* be an organization like that.''

The sheriff chewed on his bottom lip. ''I'll pretend I didn't hear that, Jennifer. I'd hate to haul you in for, for . . .''

Jennifer grinned. ''For impersonating a member of a phony organization? Well, while you're trying to decide what penal code that falls under, you can add the SCRC. The Senior Citizens' Rights Commission. I went down to the building site for the senior citizens' center, and had a to-do with the foreman.''

''And told him you're a member of the SCRC?''

''Uh-huh. He backed down when I told him I might have to close him down.''

''Jennifer!''

She shrugged. ''If I could have, I would have. The location stinks, the working conditions are deplorable, and the building materials are inferior. I don't see how it will pass inspection when it's finished. Now I have to get to work. See you both in church on Sunday?''

Their heads bobbed in unison as Jennifer went out the door.

Chapter Five

Even with Tina's help at the clinic, Saturday morning was hectic.

"Is it usually like this on Saturdays?" Tina asked when there was a lull in traffic.

"Yes," Jennifer said, pushing her hair out of her eyes. "For some, it's a necessity. When you work all week, everything falls on Saturday—the marketing, errands, and going to the vet. And then we have a few who could bring in their pets any day of the week, but have gotten into the habit. Just remember, unless it's an emergency, we don't take anybody without an appointment."

87

Tina had been working the front desk all morning, and had done a terrific job. She was good with the pet owners, and had a way with animals. And she had even handled Penelope Davis. The difficult woman had insisted Dr. Copeland, and *not* "that Gray girl" look at her cat. Somehow, Tina had managed to convince her that "that Gray girl" was a qualified veterinarian. And if she insisted on waiting for Dr. Copeland, she would have to wait all morning, because he was booked solid. She agreed to let Jennifer examine her cat, who had suddenly gained an alarming amount of weight.

"Your cat is pregnant," Jennifer told her after one quick look.

Penelope Davis's eyes grew round, and her mouth dropped open. "But she *can't* be!"

The cat was on her side on the examining table, and Jennifer smiled. "Watch her for a few moments, and you'll see the kittens moving inside her."

Penelope watched, and nearly swooned. "But she *can't* be pregnant. She never goes out. Well, sometimes she goes out, but . . .''

"It doesn't take long, Ms. Davis. I'm sure she gave you some telltale signs when she was in season, but perhaps you weren't aware of what they meant.''

Penelope mopped her forehead with a pink handkerchief. "Yowling?''

"Among other things.''

"I've always had male cats. I should never have gotten a female.''

"Are your male cats neutered?'' Jennifer asked.

Penelope scowled. "No, of course not. I would never have something awful like that done to my babies.''

It was clear Penelope Davis needed a giant lesson on animal care and responsibility, but it couldn't be done in a few minutes. Jennifer handed her a manual on cat care and said, "I would say she should have her kittens in about a week. Meanwhile, read the book, and then let nature take its course. If she has any problems, let us know.''

Penelope placed the cat in the elaborate carrier, and shook her head. "If *she* has any problems? What about me? What am *I* going to do with a litter of kittens?''

"You'll find the book more than helpful, Ms. Davis. But you may call us if you have any questions.''

"I don't suppose you can keep her here?''

"I'm sorry, but that would be impossible. This is a busy time of year for us, and we haven't the room.'' It wasn't true, of course, but this woman needed the experience first hand. Then she might realize the necessity of spaying and neutering.

"She might go the other way,'' Ben said later, while they were taking a well-deserved lunch break. "She might enjoy having those furry little critters around, and decide to breed her every season.''

"Heaven forbid.''

"Where's Tina?''

"Out in the garden eating her lunch.''

"Okay, then I can speak freely. Have you talked to the sheriff since your little visit to his office?''

"He called last night. He talked to Aldrich, and agrees with me that something is fishy. But the man is sticking to the story that the dog died of rat poison, and he buried the body. Sheriff Cody asked to see the grave site, and was met with hostility and resistance. The sheriff said he could always get a warrant, and that's when Aldrich came up with the lame story about burying the dog on the back forty, and he simply didn't have the time to make the drive.''

"And what about the wife?''

"The sheriff wanted to talk to her, but Aldrich said she was in bed with the flu. Another lame story, because Cody saw her in the living room before he knocked on the door.''

Ben finished his poached chicken breast, carefully prepared by his wife, and shuddered. "This diet is going to kill me. So now what?''

She told him about Willy's cousin and PI friend. "So now we wait and see what they can turn up. I'm going to the dance with Willy tonight, so we'll have the chance to talk.''

"Did you tell Willy that Aldrich shipped Mary's body to her parents?''

"Willy called me this morning to let me know what time he's picking me up for the party, and I told him then. He said it answered one question, at least, because she isn't buried in the Calico cemetery.''

Ben nodded. ''Speaking of the dance, I looked at the appointment book. It's going to be slow this afternoon. Why don't you call it a day and do whatever a young lady is supposed to do to get ready for a dance?''

''You don't mind?''

''Of course I don't mind. Tina will be here until three, and I'll probably close at four.''

''Well, I *do* have some shopping to do.''

''Then go. And have a good time, you hear?''

''Oh, I will. I'll catch Tina on my way out, and tell her she's in charge.''

''It's a conspiracy, that's what it is,'' Ben said, reaching for a carton of milk.

The Summer Swing dance, an annual event, was being held at the pavilion on the river. Although Jennifer had been to nearly every dance, missing only those times when she hadn't come home for summer vacation, *this* time seemed more festive.

Colorful lights and lanterns had been strung everywhere, and instead of the usual DJ, somebody had hired a three-piece combo. Somebody had gone overboard on the food too—the spread on the buffet table looked scrumptious.

Aware that the summer dance was changing right along with the town, Jennifer felt a stab of melancholy.

"If I tell you that's a terrific dress, and you're the prettiest gal here, will it put a smile on your face?" Willy asked, giving her a hug.

"It'll help bunches," Jennifer said, smiling up at him. "You look pretty spiffy too. New suit?"

"Nah, just some old thing I had in the closet."

She smoothed down a lapel. "It looks expensive to me."

"Well, this is a special night. You're finally home, where you belong."

It was a sweet thing to say, and Jennifer swallowed the lump in her throat. "Who planned the dance? I assume you still have a committee?"

"We do, though Sara had the final say."

Jennifer looked around. "I don't see her, or Mike, for that matter."

"They left for Omaha this morning. Sara's grandmother is ill."

Jennifer sighed. "Time certainly has a way of getting away from us, doesn't it? Sara is my best friend, and I've only seen her twice since I've been home."

"That's life, Jennifer. Times change, things change. But it doesn't mean we don't care. Do you want to dance or eat?"

"Both, and I don't care in what order. I just want to have a good time, Willy, and forget about everything but this wonderful night. I want to float on my lovely memories, and my dreams of the future."

"Why didn't you tell me sooner?" Jennifer demanded.

"Because you would've gotten all worked up, like you're doing now, and said nuts to the dance. So what's a couple of hours? We've had a good time, Jennifer, and sometimes that can be pretty important," Willy reminded her.

They had left the dance and were walking near the duck pond. Although they could still see the lights from the pavilion and hear the music, they were very much alone. It would have been romantic, if Willy hadn't said, "My cousin called this morning, and Deke, my PI buddy, called this afternoon."

"I know, and I'm sorry. And you're right. What's a couple of hours? So what did they say?"

"Norm, my cousin, found Mary's parents in Bismarck. Her father owns half the town. I guess it about broke their hearts when Mary married Aldrich. They called him a drifter, but admitted he was charming. And their daughter was inexperienced. He swept her off her feet. The father was so distraught he threatened to take away her inheritance."

Jennifer felt a chill down her spine. "Inheritance?"

"Yeah, but he didn't. I know what you're thinking, but it doesn't wash. She would only get the inheritance if the parents were dead. But there was another, smaller inheritance she received from her grandmother. There was nothing they could do about that."

"How much?"

"Five hundred grand."

"Whoa! And did the money go to Aldrich after Mary died?" Jennifer asked eagerly.

"It did, along with a sizable insurance policy."

"What about the death certificate?"

"Signed by a Dr. Lewis in North Platte. Supposedly Mary died of a massive coronary. At least that's the way it reads. When I talked to the doctor, he was pretty emphatic. No, he didn't perform an autopsy, but she had all the classic signs, postmortem. And she'd had some heart problems before."

"I know it's been a long time, but maybe if we can get the body exhumed . . ."

"Aldrich had Mary cremated in North Platte, and sent the remains home to her parents in an urn. They were livid, but there wasn't anything they could do."

"Convenient," Jennifer noted wryly.

"Yeah, and it was almost a repeat performance of the first marriage, only with a few added twists. Deke found Addy Allison's mother in Sioux Falls. The father is dead—died before Addy married Aldrich, so she already had her inheritance.''

''Uh-huh. Money in that family too?''

''Lots of it,'' Willy said emphatically.

''And suddenly Addy died.''

''Drowned in Spirit Lake. They'd been married about a year, and were on a vacation. Aldrich claimed Addy went for an early morning swim, and never came back. When they found her body, there were no signs of foul play.''

Jennifer took a deep breath. ''And the few added twists?''

''The mother claims Addy was an excellent swimmer. Even had some medals. And here's the best one. Richard Aldrich was born and raised in Sioux Falls. He went to school with Addy, but they didn't date until their senior year. Then it was an on-again, off-again thing for a while. The mother says it was a volatile relationship. Addy was beautiful, and Aldrich was jealous. Aldrich's mother died shortly after he was born, and he lived with his father on the family farm. It was quite a spread.''

''So he had money.''

"Sounds like it. After the father died, Aldrich and Addy got married and lived on the farm. The vacation at Spirit Lake was the first they had taken since the honeymoon."

"And they went on the vacation alone?"

"As far as anybody knows."

"And after Addy died?"

"Aldrich sold the farm and moved away. Rumor was, he moved to Des Moines, and Deke dug a little deeper. Aldrich bought a ranch near Des Moines, and married Estelle Miller. Influence, money, and a huge insurance policy came with that one. She died a year later. It was an accident too. They were in 'Little Switzerland,' and she fell off a bluff into the Mississippi River. He sold the ranch a few months later, and moved on. That's where the trail ends, until he popped up in Calico."

It was quite a story, and it left Jennifer speechless.

Willy went on. "So, I think it's safe to say we have a pattern. Marry them rich and kill them off."

Jennifer suddenly felt icy cold, and hugged her arms close to her body. "He's a monster, Willy. And now I'm more convinced than ever he's trying to kill Pam.''

"For sure. You haven't said, but does Pam have money?''

"I have no idea, but I'm going to find out. Did you find out who sold him the ranch?''

"Yes. Treemont, the first owner, left it in the hands of a North Platte realtor. I made a few calls, and tracked him down. It was a cash sale.''

"And now Aldrich is in financial difficulty. That adds to the pattern, Willy, if Pam has money.''

"It also addresses the question, why is he broke? Two years ago, he had it all— five thousand head of cattle, and impressive stud fees. He owned the ranch free and clear, so you tell me.''

"Somehow, some way, I have to talk to Pam. I also have to talk to the sheriff, and as soon as possible,'' Jennifer said firmly.

"You want to call him tonight? I have his home phone number.''

"I think we'd better. I hate to say it, but I don't think we have a moment to lose.''

* * *

They were seated in the sheriff's comfortable living room, with cups of coffee and a plate of cookies. Jim Cody listened to the incredible story that encompassed nearly twenty years, and shook his head. "I hear you, and I agree, but we can't arrest the man on speculation or suspicion. One wife died of a heart attack, and two wives died in tragic accidents. If nobody suspected him then, nobody is gonna suspect him now."

"But *we* do," Jennifer insisted. "And that has to count for something."

"Yeah, overactive imaginations. Without some kind of proof, we're dead in the water."

When Jennifer shuddered at his terminology, the sheriff tightened the belt on his robe and sighed. "I'm sorry, but it's the truth."

Jennifer took a deep breath. "Somehow, I have to talk to Pam alone. Maybe if I can get her to open up, I'll find the right spot to tell her she's in danger. I know she's frightened, so maybe it wouldn't take much."

Willy finished off a cookie and wiped his

mouth on a paper napkin. "What if you pick Aldrich up for questioning, Jim? Use the dog poisoning as an excuse if you have to, but if you can manage to keep him in your office long enough, Jennifer can go out to the ranch and —"

The sheriff grunted. "It wouldn't work. There is no way I could legally bring him in because of the dog. I'd be in deep trouble. You know that, Willy. I don't know why you're even suggesting it."

"Sometimes desperate situations mean desperate choices."

Jennifer opened her mouth, and the sheriff raised a hand. "I know what you're going to say, Jennifer, but don't. There is no way that lamebrain RCQ-whatever would wash."

Jennifer shrugged. "It might. Did you mention it to him when you talked to him?"

"No, and I wasn't about to."

"Well, now is your chance. I set him up, and you can tighten the screws, so to speak. What can he do, go to the sheriff?"

Sheriff Cody added an extra spoonful of

sugar to his coffee, and stirred it vigorously. "He can go to the mayor."

"And so the mayor tells him he's never heard of the ACRARQCO. I say, big deal. Mayor Attwater had never heard of the Keya Paha Big Game Refuge either, and it's in our county."

"How did you find that out?" Willy asked.

"Because I asked him what he thought of it one day at church. He looked at me like I was speaking in a foreign language. That's the way he is about everything. If it isn't on his desk in front of him, forget it. His term is up next year, and I have the feeling he won't get reelected."

The sheriff grinned. "Is this you talking, Jennifer, or your grandfather? The mayor is also behind the shove for more commerce, and we all know how your grandfather feels about that."

Jennifer lifted her chin. "I share my grandfather's views on a lot of things, but that's sidestepping the issue."

Cody scratched his head. "I'd never be able to remember the ACRA . . ."

"You would if it was written down. I'll

tell you what. I'll list some questions you can ask him, and put the name of the so-called organization right on top. You won't be able to miss it. With enough questions, you might be able to detain him for a couple of hours, and that's all I'll need.''

''It's crazy.''

''Maybe, but think how good you'll feel if we can save Pam's life.''

''Have you thought about what might happen if you're wrong?''

''Do you think I'm wrong?''

''To tell you the truth, I don't know what to think. But I took an oath to uphold the law, and I guess that's what I'd better do. When do you want to do this?''

''Tomorrow morning. Grandfather already knows I won't be at church because we have a lot of cleanup at the clinic. It's always that way after a busy Saturday.''

''So what about the clinic?''

''They'll survive without me for a couple of hours. We have a new girl, and she's a sweetheart. Call me at the clinic when you get Aldrich to your office, and I'll head for the ranch.''

The sheriff rolled his eyes. ''Yeah, right.

I'm supposed to call you in front of him and say, 'We're here, Jennifer, settled down in the office for a two-hour talk. So you can go do your thing.' "

"I think you can use a little more imagination than that. Pretend you're calling your wife, and tell her you'll be home for lunch."

Willy grinned, and a dimple creased his cheek. "Can you believe this lady is the pastor's granddaughter?" he asked the sheriff.

"Yeah, I can, as a matter of fact, because this is exactly the kind of thing old Wes would've done before he got his calling. I knew him way back when, and I can tell you a story or two."

Jennifer gave both men a brilliant smile. "Then it's settled?"

"Yeah, but I ain't getting up before eight," Cody groused.

"I'll stick the list of questions through your office mail slot on my way to the clinic in the morning. How's that?"

"That's against the law," he muttered. "Nothing is supposed to go in the mail slot except mail."

Jennifer blew him a kiss as they headed for the door.

Outside, Jennifer breathed in deeply of the sweet night air. "I'd ask you to come with me tomorrow, Willy, but I think Pam will be more responsive if I'm alone."

"I understand, but promise me you'll be careful?"

"I'm always careful," she replied coyly, and looped an arm through his.

Chapter Six

Jennifer woke up the next morning to the sound of the squeaking treadmill. At first she thought she was hearing things. It was only five-thirty, and although both Emma and her grandfather were early risers, this was almost too early even for them. It took a few minutes to get her feet on the floor, and then she crept down the hall.

Expecting to find her grandfather on the treadmill, she couldn't have been more surprised to see Emma, wearing warm-ups, walking the road that lead nowhere. And she was doing a bang-up job. Jennifer watched for a few minutes before she cleared her throat.

Emma turned around and flushed. "Well, it's here, isn't it?" she said defensively, turning off the machine.

"Hey, I think it's great, Emma, and don't stop on my account."

Emma blew at a puff of hair that had blown over her face. "I'm stopping because I want to."

Jennifer stepped into the room. "There is one thing, Emma, and it's important. I know Grandfather got the okay to exercise from Dr. Chambers, but what about you?"

"I saw Doc Chambers on Friday, and he said I can do what I want, if I use moderation. It was his way of telling me I'm an old lady, and I have to be careful. What's that for?" She pointed at the balance bar, resting against one wall.

"I use it for stretching exercises, but you can also use it for balance."

"And that?"

"It's called a rowing machine."

"Like in a boat, huh?"

"Sort of. Want me to show you how everything works?"

Emma shook her head. "Not now. I have to take a shower and get breakfast on the table. Your grandfather wants waffles and strawberry jam. Three eggs too, and those little sausages. He expects a full house for the services this morning, and needs a kick into high gear. Well, of course I need some energy too, after all this work."

Jennifer groaned inwardly. What they both needed was a sensible diet to go along with a simple exercise program, but now wasn't the time to get into it, especially when she knew she was going to be met with opposition. And she wanted to be at the clinic by eight, and get as much work done as possible before the sheriff called.

"Are you okay?" Emma asked, watching Jennifer intently. "You look a little pale. Too much party last night?"

"No. The party was wonderful. And now I have to get going too. I have a big day planned."

"And I suppose all you're going to eat is a piece of toast?" Emma grunted derisively.

"Not even that, Emma. But I'll eat later, I promise."

Emma shook her head, and marched out.

Jennifer did a quick round on the stationary bike, and headed for her room. What she really had to do was finish the list of questions for the sheriff.

At ten minutes after ten, Sheriff Cody called. Ben let Jennifer take it, because he knew what was going on, but the concern on his face was obvious.

"This is it," she whispered, after she hung up. "I'll tell Tina I have to go out on a house call."

Ben was disinfecting the holding cages, and gave one an extra swipe with the rag. "Some house call. I don't like this, Jennifer, and I don't care who the heck knows it."

"I don't like it either," Jennifer admitted, "but it has to be done. I won't be much longer than a couple of hours."

"We'll probably get everything done in a couple more hours."

"Okay, then I'll work extra hours next week to make up the time."

Ben tossed aside the rag. "It's not the hours or the time. I don't give a diddly-

squat about that. I'm worried about *you.*
What if the sheriff can't keep the creep
long enough? What if Aldrich goes home
and finds you talking to his wife? Or worse,
snooping around?''

''Then I guess I'll just have to wing it,''
Jennifer said, taking off her smock. ''Wish
me luck?''

He gave her a hug. ''I wish for a lot
more than that, young lady. If I'm not here
when you get back, will you call me at
home?''

''I will. Promise.''

But as Jennifer made her way to the
Jeep, she was sorry she'd made the prom-
ise. She had already broken the promise to
Emma; she hadn't had anything to eat.

By the time Jennifer pulled up in the
gravel parking area, her stomach was tied
in a knot, and it wasn't because she was
hungry. What if she couldn't convince Pam
Aldrich she was in danger? Worse, what if
the woman slammed the door in her face?
There was a fine line here, and walking it
wouldn't be easy. She was playing with
lives. She had no proof Richard Aldrich

was a killer, and so she would have to wait for a sign. What sign? A sign from God that it was okay to meddle?

Jennifer took a deep breath and headed for the house. No, she would have to wait for a sign from Pam Aldrich that she was willing to pour out her heart. She prayed for forgiveness not only for meddling, but for the lies she was going to have to tell.

Pam opened the door on the second knock, and stepped back as though she'd been stricken. "I-I wasn't expecting you," she mumbled.

Jennifer managed a smile. "I know, and I'm sorry for the intrusion, but if I could have a few moments of your time . . ."

Pam glanced at her watch, and opened the door another inch. "What do you want to talk to me about?"

"Bart."

"The sheriff was already here."

"I don't know anything about that, but I thought you would like to know that Bart received a proper burial."

This time the door opened, and Pam stood aside. "Come in."

The inside of the house wasn't anything

like Jennifer expected. It was filled with touches of warmth, and flowers spilled over in vases everywhere. There was little doubt Pam had tried to make the ranch house a home. It was also easy to see she was nervous—even jumpy.

Pam motioned toward a leather chair. "If you'd like to sit down . . ."

Jennifer sat down, and waited until Pam was seated on the tweed couch, before she said, "I found Bart's body, and had him buried at the pet cemetery near the river. I thought you would like to know."

"I-I don't understand."

"The last time I was here, your husband told me Bart had died, and that he had buried the body. I also had the front door slammed in my face."

"I know, and I'm so sorry."

"It doesn't matter. What matters is the fact that I saw vultures circling around after I left that day. I went to investigate. You have to understand, Mrs. Aldrich. I'm a veterinarian, and if I come across a wounded animal, *any* wounded animal, I have to do what I can."

"You found Bart, and he was wounded?"

"I found Bart, and he was dead. Somebody had shot him through the head and tossed him into a gully."

Jennifer waited for that to sink in before going on, but she couldn't ignore the tears in the woman's eyes. "I couldn't leave him there, so I took him to the clinic. Dr. Copeland removed the bullet for evidence, and I called the pet cemetery. I have the plot number, if you would like to visit it."

The woman was twisting her hands in her lap. "Who paid for it?"

"I did, and Dr. Copeland kicked in."

"I'll have to reimburse you . . ."

"I would rather have some answers. First of all, who shot Bart?"

"Somebody with a sick mind."

"I agree, but who?"

"Will he get into trouble? You mentioned the bullet . . ."

"Truthfully, I don't know."

"Is that the reason Richard had to go with the sheriff this morning? Does the sheriff think Richard shot Bart?"

"Did he?"

''No, one of the ranch hands shot him.''

''What is the ranch hand's name?''

Pam hesitated, and then said, ''Jeb Tyler. It . . . it was terrible. I wanted to keep Bart in the house, but Richard wouldn't hear of it. So I made a bed in the barn. I used one of our good sheets and a blanket, and Richard had a fit. We argued. Tyler was there, and said he would end the dispute once and for all. We were in the barn . . .'' She closed her eyes, trying to hold back the tears. ''I can still hear the shot.''

Jennifer took a deep breath. ''What did your husband say? What did he do?''

''He didn't say anything. He muttered something under his breath, tossed Bart in the back of his truck, and drove away.''

''Without reprimanding Tyler?''

''Nobody reprimands Tyler.''

''Does Tyler usually solve things with a gun?''

''I-I don't know what you mean.''

''It just seems strange to me that a man who is supposedly dedicated to veterinary medicine, would shoot an innocent animal.''

''You know Tyler?''

"I've heard of him."

Pam looked away. "Tyler isn't dedicated to anything unless there is something in it for him." She shook her head. "I'm sorry, I'm not being a very good hostess. Would you like something to drink? I have a special blend of tea, and the water is hot."

"I'm not a tea drinker, Mrs. Aldrich. But I'll take a glass of ice water."

When Pam headed for the kitchen, Jennifer was right behind her. There was no way she was going to leave the woman alone.

After Pam poured water into a tall glass and filled it with ice, Jennifer asked, "Where is Tyler now?"

"Out on the range repairing fences, I guess. I haven't seen him all morning."

Jennifer took the glass and sat down at the table. "How many ranch hands does your husband employ?"

"He had fifteen until . . ."

"Until he sold off most of his stock?"

Pam dropped into a chair. "How did you find out about that?"

"You've only been married a short time, and you rarely come into town. If you were more familiar with Calico, you would know it's full of warm, caring people who make it a point to know about their neighbors. Some might think it means being snoopy, but it really isn't. It's genuine concern. Your husband has always been a recluse, and that also makes him an enigma. So how many ranch hands does he have now?''

''Five, and Tyler.''

''I understand Tyler has been working here a long time.''

''Too long, according to Richard. They don't get along.''

''Then why doesn't your husband fire him?''

''To tell you the truth, I don't know.''

''Is he really a veterinarian?''

''He says he is, but I doubt it. When an animal is ill or injured, he doesn't take care of it, he shoots it.''

Jennifer shivered. ''He doesn't sound like a very nice man.''

''He isn't . . .''

Perspiration had popped out on Pam's forehead, and her hands were trembling.

"Are you ill?" Jennifer asked, suddenly concerned.

"I've been feeling out of sorts for a few weeks, but it comes and goes, so I don't think it's anything serious."

"Have you seen a doctor?"

Pam shook her head. "Richard says the doctor in town is a quack, and North Platte is too far to go."

"It isn't *that* far, if you're truly ill."

Pam waved a hand. "Like I said, it comes and goes."

Jennifer looked around the kitchen. "This is a nice house, and you've done a good job with the decorating."

"It's what I did before we got married."

"Decorating?"

"Interior design for a company in St. Paul."

"Minnesota?"

"Yes. I was born and raised there."

"Is that where you met your husband?"

"No, I was visiting my sister in Boston. Richard was there on vacation. Well, actually, he said he was mixing business with pleasure. We were staying at the same hotel, and met in the lounge. He was so good-looking, and charming. And then when he said he was a rancher . . .''

"That impressed you?"

"He was wearing beautiful leather boots, tight jeans and a felt Stetson. That impressed me, and the fact that he knew how to show a lady a good time. He told me that first night he was a widower. The way he talked about Mary broke my heart. It was so sad. That day I brought Bart to the clinic, you said you knew her."

"I knew her, but we weren't good friends. She rarely left the ranch, for one thing."

Pam looked away. "Well, I can understand that. Richard has a thing about women having independence. He believes a wife should stay at home where she belongs."

"And are you comfortable with that?"

"I loved him so much, it didn't bother me at first, but now . . . Excuse me for a moment while I fix my tea."

Jennifer watched the slump to the woman's shoulders as she filled a mug with hot water. She concentrated on drawing the courage to ask the next question. When

Pam finally turned around, she said, "That day you brought Bart to the clinic, you told me the strychnine was in the hamburger, and that it had been meant for you. Is there a reason why you said that?"

"I-I was upset."

"Yes, of course you were, but that was a pretty heavy statement. So heavy, in fact, I haven't been able to get it out of my mind. You all but implied that somebody is trying to kill you. I could have gone to the sheriff."

Pam's hand flew up to her mouth. "That . . . that isn't why the sheriff picked Richard up this morning, is it? Oh, no, you didn't tell the sheriff!"

"No, I didn't tell Sheriff Cody. You seem terribly frightened, Mrs. Aldrich. You keep looking at your watch. Are you afraid your husband is going to come home and find me here?"

"He . . . he doesn't like me to have company."

"What about your family?"

"My family didn't approve of the marriage. I haven't seen or talked to them in nearly a year."

Jennifer shook her head. "This whole thing sounds like it's right out of the Dark Ages, Pam. Do you mind if I call you Pam?"

"No. And I know what you must be thinking, but you don't know Richard. He's a jealous man, and has a terrible temper. I loved him so much, and now . . . I didn't know him. He's not the man I thought I married."

"Then why don't you leave?"

"He said if I ever left him, he'd kill me."

The time was now. Jennifer gripped the glass. "Maybe he's trying to kill you anyway. And maybe you know it. Maybe that's why you thought there was strychnine in the hamburger." Pam opened her mouth to reply, but Jennifer pressed on. "I think you should know Mary wasn't his first wife. She was his third wife, and you're the fourth."

Pam sucked in her breath.

"I realize it must be a shock, but you have the right to know. His first wife drowned in a lake, even though she was a good swimmer. His second wife fell off a bluff and into the Mississippi River. The tragedies were called 'accidents.' The third wife, Mary, was ill for a long time, and supposedly died of a heart attack.''

Pam swayed, and her face was pale. ''How did you find out about his wives?''

''I had some friends do some checking. All of his wives came from money, and had healthy life insurance policies. Can I assume that scenario fits you as well?''

Pam took a deep, ragged breath. ''I have money, but it's in a special trust. I can't touch it without my father's approval.''

''Did your husband know that when he married you?''

''No. After he brought me to the ranch, he said he was in financial trouble, and needed some money. When he found out I couldn't get to my money, he was livid.''

''Did he ever tell you why he was in financial trouble?''

''No.''

''And what happens to the money if you die?''

''He can't touch it.''

''Insurance?'' Jennifer prodded.

''Yes. A fifty-thousand-dollar policy I've

had since I was small, and one for a hundred thousand that Richard took out after we were married.''

''And the trust fund?''

''A million and some change.''

Pam was seated in the chair again, and Jennifer reached over and patted her hand. ''Whether you want to believe it or not, Pam, I *am* your friend. And I want to help. If your husband is a murderer, he has to be put away. I was born and raised in Calico, and just the thought of having a killer on the loose . . .'' She shook her head. ''I know that sounds terrible, and I'm so sorry. But I truly believe your life is in danger. Now, if you'll level with me. . . . ''

''We . . . we had a terrible fight one night. He was drunk, and said he was going to feed me rat poison and put me out of my misery. I didn't believe him until Bart ate the hamburger patty.''

''But you have to realize that if he put poison in the hamburger and you had died, he would have been the number one suspect. I have a hard time with that, because I think he's smarter than that. Tell me the truth. What did you do with the hamburger?''

''I left it on the counter. After I came home from the clinic, Richard gave me what-for. He said I wasted good money, leaving the hamburger out like that. He threw it out.'' Pam was shivering uncontrollably. ''Oh, Jennifer, what do I do?''

''You let me take you to North Platte, so you can catch the first plane to St. Paul.''

''That would be the first place he would look. He said if I left him he'd kill me, and I believe him. Sometime, someplace, I'd have an accident, and end up conveniently dead.''

''Then let me take you to town. I'll find some place for you to hide, and—''

Pam ran a hand through her titian hair. ''And what would that accomplish? I have no proof that he wants to kill me, and if he's gotten away with it before . . .''

Pam had a point, and it sent Jennifer's thoughts into a whirl. ''Then we have to get proof. I'll talk to the sheriff. I guess I'd better tell you—I lied to you. The sheriff knows everything. He picked up your husband this morning on the pretense of questioning him about Bart. Feeble, I know, but I wanted a chance to talk to you alone. He's going to try to keep your husband detained for a couple of hours.''

Pam fought back tears and looked at her watch. ''Time is almost up.''

''I know. I'll take one of the back roads so I don't pass him along the way. I don't want him to know I've been talking to you. Look, if you think you can handle things here, I'll talk to the sheriff and see if we can come up with a plan. Meanwhile, try to act normal, and whatever you do, don't leave the house. I'll give you the phone number at the clinic and the number at my house, but if I want to call you—''

''Richard is always out on the range between eight and eleven.''

''Then that's when I'll call.''

The tears finally rolled down Pam's cheeks. ''This is a nightmare,'' she said miserably.

''I know, but we have a big plus on our side. You're still alive.''

Jennifer took the back roads to town, and headed for the sheriff's department. She prayed they wouldn't run out of time.

Chapter Seven

Jennifer parked the Cherokee down the block from the sheriff's department, in the event Richard Aldrich was still with Cody. and slipped in the back way. She was in the supply room, and the door to the office was open a crack. She could hear loud voices, and held her breath while she listened to their parting words. "I've arranged for one of my deputies to drive you home, but you'd better be watching over your shoulder, Aldrich. We don't take kindly to animal killers around here," the sheriff was saying.

"Yeah, well, you and the RCRAR, or

whatever the heck it is, can expect a lawsuit on your hands. I don't take kindly to being harassed!'' Aldrich's voice was venomous.

She waited until she heard the front door slam, and slipped into the office. The sheriff was wiping the perspiration off his brow with a handkerchief, and Nettie was banging things around. ''I take it, it didn't go well?'' Jennifer asked softly.

Sheriff Cody looked at her and sighed. ''Well, now I can breathe a little easier. Your two hours were up a half hour ago, and I didn't know what to do. I couldn't hold him any longer . . . Don't want to go through that again, young lady.''

''Hopefully, you won't have to. Did you spend the whole time arguing with him?''

''*He* did most of the arguing,'' Nettie muttered. ''I wanted Jim to throw him in jail.''

Jim Cody sat down behind his desk and loosened his tie. ''So you'd better tell me these last two-and-a-half miserable hours were worth it.''

''Believe me, they were. I had a long talk with Pam, and she finally opened up.

She told me they'd had a fight one night, and he told her he was going to feed her rat poison and put her out of her misery. He was drunk, but she believed him, and then when the dog was poisoned . . .''

"Did Aldrich shoot the dog?"

"No, it was Jeb Tyler, the hired hand who claims he is a vet."

"Some vet." The sheriff snorted.

"That's what I said. I tried to talk her into coming into town with me, but she refused. She also brought up a good point. She doesn't have one shred of evidence that Aldrich is trying to kill her, so we have to come up with a plan."

The sheriff shook his head. "This isn't a television show, Jennifer. This is reality. I haven't got one blasted reason to lock him up, and the lady doesn't have a leg to stand on. It goes right back to conjecture and gut feelings. And it's a wash."

"I take it you didn't get anything out of him?"

"No, and I've gotta tell you, I've grilled known felons with a lot less enthusiasm. I'm afraid he's gonna have to make an actual attempt on her life before I can do any-thing.''

''Maybe if you pick *her* up for question-ing, he'll get so upset he'll make a mistake. No, better scratch that. I have the feeling he would take it out on her.''

''He might anyway. He was pretty upset when he left.''

''Then it's a no-win situation,'' Jennifer said dismally.

''Unless you can get her to leave town. Hey, so what if he's threatened her? The world is a big place. Lots of places to hide.''

''And she would be looking over her shoulder for the rest of her life. Do you think he'll sue?''

''You heard that, huh? Not if he's guilty. Look, this has been a rotten morning, and I'm ready for a break. I promised my wife I'd go home for lunch, and that's where I'm headed. A late lunch is better than no lunch. I'm sorry this didn't work out, Jen-nifer, but like I told Aldrich, 'big daddy' will be watching. That was a bunch of bunk too, but maybe it will keep him in line.''

''I don't believe that for one minute,''

Jennifer said, feeling her stomach cramp in hunger at the mention of lunch. "I have to call Ben and Willy."

The sheriff nodded toward the phone, and began straightening up the papers on his desk.

Kelly's Coffee Shop had lost most of the lunch crowd by the time Jennifer walked through the door, and she was grateful for that, at least. And then she spotted Elmer Dodd in a back booth, and fought with her emotions. Did she want to fight with the man on a full or empty stomach? She decided she didn't want to fight with him at all. At least not now. Too much was happening, and she was too upset to deal with him. *Later,* she told herself, sitting down at the counter. Later, after she knew Pam was safe, and Richard Aldrich was behind bars.

Sally, a pretty, plump waitress who had been working at Kelly's forever, gave Jennifer a broad smile. "Hi, Jennifer. Welcome home. What will it be?"

Jennifer returned the waitress's smile. "Thanks, Sally, it's good to be home. I'll have a tuna melt on rye, no dressing, and a glass of iced tea.''

"I heard you were back in town.'' The gruff, unpleasant voice came from Elmer Dodd, strolling by on his way to the cashier. "And Digger Meehan said you were already poking around. It didn't take you long to find somebody to pick on, did it?''

Jennifer sighed. It would seem that a confrontation with the despicable man wasn't going to wait. She turned around to glare at him, and felt the usual wave of revulsion. He was short and fat, with a head of dark slicked-back hair, and black, piercing eyes. He also had his infamous cigar in his hand. She tried to concentrate on his yellow teeth instead of his sizable belly, and said, "Would you like to tell me why you gave our senior citizens a plot of arid land near the refuse disposal site, and all that substandard lumber?''

"The land was just sitting there, and the old folks were happy to get it,'' he said gruffly.

"Yes, because nobody offered them anything better,'' she countered

"And the lumber isn't substandard.''

"The structure will never pass inspection."

"Oh, yes it will," he said, waving his cigar for effect.

Jennifer's brow furrowed. "So who do you have in your pocket? The mayor? The planning commission? The town council?"

"That's not a very nice thing to say, Jennifer, but I should have expected it. You're just like your father."

"Don't you *dare* bring my father into this!"

"Why not? He had a knack for stirring up trouble too. Big crusader."

Jennifer lifted her chin. "He found out you were altering the freshness dates on your dairy products, Mr. Dodd—products way over the expiration date, that should have been thrown out. He had no choice but to report it."

"He reported it because he didn't understand about profit and loss. He wasn't a businessman. He was only the town pharmacist who thought he was above everyone. He was that way in school too—big man on campus. Always looking for a cause."

"He was also an honest man, Mr. Dodd. Can you look in the mirror and say the same thing? You're not going to get away with this. Someday, you're going to have to answer to what you've done to our senior citizens."

"And someday, I'm going to be mayor. Then we'll see who has the last laugh."

Jennifer sucked in her breath. "You're going to run for mayor?"

"You'd better believe it, little lady. And I have over half the town behind me."

Jennifer wiped her sweaty palms on her skirt. "The election is a year away. Anything can happen."

"That's right, so you best be looking over your shoulder."

Disgusted, Jennifer turned away from him, and sipped the tea Sally had placed in front of her. Did he indeed have half the town behind him? Or did he actually have half the town in his pocket?

A few minutes later, Elmer Dodd paid his tab and left the coffee shop, but not before Jennifer had seen the malevolent smile on his face.

*   *   *

"Forget about him, Jennifer," Wes said that night at dinner. "He'd like to think he's a lot bigger than he is."

"And if he gets elected?"

"He won't."

Jennifer picked at the macaroni and cheese on her plate. "How can you be so sure?"

Wes grinned. "Because you're going to see to it he doesn't. You're made of tough stuff, Jennifer, and I'm proud to have you as a granddaughter. You're just like your daddy."

"That's what Elmer Dodd said."

"Good! Maybe it'll give him something to think about. Your daddy was a fine man, and fought hard for law and justice."

"Maybe he should have been a cop instead of a pharmacist."

"He thought about it, but, like you, he made his decision. I know he never regretted it."

Emma clucked her tongue. "Nobody is eating."

Jennifer opened her mouth, and then closed it. Now wasn't the time to tell Emma the food on her plate was probably worth several thousand calories, or that she'd had a late lunch and wasn't hungry. Nor were her thoughts on Elmer Dodd. She was thinking about Pam, and prayed she would be safe for at least one more night.

" 'Fess up," Wes said, sliding into the pew beside Jennifer. "I saw you sneaking into the church after dinner. Thought maybe I should leave you alone, but then I reconsidered. Your problems are my problems, and they always will be."

Jennifer managed a smile. "I missed the service this morning, and I thought I'd try to make up for it."

"Nope, you can't fool me. I watched you trying to choke down dinner. One missed service doesn't cut it. Is it Elmer Dodd?"

"Yes . . . no—I don't know, Grandfather. I stirred up a hornet's nest, and now . . ."

"With Dodd? Maybe I should tell you about the time—"

"No, not with Elmer Dodd," Jennifer interrupted. "Well, that too, but he's not the problem at the moment. I went to see

Pam Aldrich this morning. She opened up to me, and what she had to say is really scary.''

Wes took a deep breath. ''Where was Aldrich?''

''We devised a plan . . . Well, *I* thought it up. Sheriff Cody picked him up for questioning regarding the dog poisoning. It was a ruse to get him away from the ranch, so I could talk to Pam.''

''And here I thought you were at the clinic all day.''

''I was only there until a little after ten. The sheriff detained Aldrich for over two hours, which gave me plenty of time to get to the ranch and talk to Pam. It's really a mess, and I don't know what to do about it. One of the hired hands shot the dog, and Aldrich has threatened to kill Pam if she leaves him. She told me he's jealous, has a terrible temper, and she's scared to death of him. I told her about his other wives.''

''Don't you think you should let Sheriff Cody handle it?''

''He doesn't know what to do any more than I do. And for every hour Pam spends with that man . . . I think he's planning to kill her too, Grandfather. I think he killed all his wives, and she's next on his list. She has a trust fund she can't touch without her father's approval, but she also has one hundred and fifty thousand dollars in life insurance. If Aldrich needs money . . .''

Wes ran a hand through his white hair. ''If she's that frightened, why doesn't she leave?''

''I tried to talk her into leaving, but she's afraid he'll come after her.''

''He sounds like a sick man.''

''He is, but that doesn't help. Not if he's a killer. I don't know that much about the criminal mind, but if he feels threatened, who knows what he might do.''

''What does Sheriff Cody say?''

''Not much. Without proof, his hands are tied. He said there will have to be an attempt on Pam's life before he can do anything. But what if it isn't just an attempt? What if Aldrich succeeds? And I can't help but wonder how he plans to do it. His first wife drowned, his second wife fell off a bluff into the Mississippi River, and Mary supposedly died of a heart attack. But did she? The doctor in North Platte who signed the death certificate swears she died of a massive coronary. Maybe that's what it looked like, but what if? And did Aldrich have her body cremated to cover up the truth?''

''Maybe you should have the collie's body exhumed and perform an autopsy,'' Wes suggested.

''And what would that prove? We know the dog ingested strychnine, and we know he ate the hamburger, but even if we had performed an autopsy right after he died, it would have been too late to determine if the strychnine was in the hamburger. He lived nearly twenty-four hours after the poisoning, and the hamburger would have passed through his system. But the thing is, I still have a hard time believing Aldrich would have done something that blatant, or that unpredictable. He had no way of knowing the amount of hamburger Pam would eat. If it wasn't enough, it wouldn't have killed her. I don't think he would have left it to chance, Grandfather. He would have been much more thorough than that. I think my original impression was accurate. The dog ingested rat poison somewhere on the ranch. I think the fact that he ate the hamburger was merely coincidence.''

''So where do you go from here?''

''I have no idea, but I'm going to keep trying to talk Pam into getting away from him. She said the best time to call her is between eight and eleven in the morning. That's when Aldrich is out on the range, and I'll make the first call in the morning. And I'll call her the next morning, and the next. Hopefully, I'll get through to her. And at least by keeping in contact with her, I'll know she's still alive.''

Wes gave her a hug. ''Want to be alone for a while?''

''No, I want you to hold my hand and pray with me. I need your strength and love.''

Wes gave her hand a squeeze, and lowered his head.

Jennifer heard the squeaking treadmill at seven, but she'd been awake for hours, going over everything in her mind. Somehow, she'd missed something. A clue? A tiny shred of evidence? Something somebody had said? Something somebody had done? She knew it was right at her fingertips, yet it remained as elusive as a foggy dream.

Jennifer sat up amid the tangle of sheets, and ran a hand through her hair. She felt headachy and shaky, out of sorts. She was wondering how she was going to get through the day, when she remembered the perspiration that had suddenly popped out on Pam's forehead, her trembling hands, and her words: "I've been feeling out of sorts for a few weeks, but it comes and goes, so I don't think it's anything serious." She also remembered Mary, ice-cold and trembling, and the "bug" she said she couldn't seem to shake.

Jennifer's heart was pounding in her ears as she slipped into her jeans and blouse. *Arsenic poisoning!* Abdominal pains, vomiting, staggering, trembling, coldness in the extremities, and eventual internal damage and paralysis. Possibly, a heart attack. Arsenic was one of the fast-acting poisons, but it could also be administered in small doses. Accumulative, it was just as deadly as a single massive dose. And there was something else . . . She shook her head. It had been the flash of a thought.

Jennifer walked to the exercise room on shaky legs, waited until Emma turned off the treadmill, and said, "That episode of *Murder She Wrote*—you know, the one about the arsenic poisoning. How did the killer do it?''

Emma wiped her face with a towel, and raised a brow. "Why, he was putting it in his wife's coffee. He wasn't a coffee drinker, and—''

Jennifer swayed and grabbed the balance bar. Mary had been a tea drinker, and so was Pam! Pam had even mentioned her "special'' blend. Both women had offered Jennifer tea, and she had declined. Was that one of the reasons Richard Aldrich didn't want company at the ranch? Was he afraid a guest might get a dose of tainted tea?

"I think you're coming down with something, young lady,'' Emma said stoutly. "Best we get you back to bed, and—''

Jennifer tried for a smile. "I'm not ill, Emma. I simply have a lot on my mind. Is Grandfather up?''

"Not yet."

"Then tell him I'll see him later."

"You're leaving now?"

"I have a lot to do this morning, and I want to get an early start."

She gave Emma a hug and hurried out, barely able to contain her excitement.

Jim Cody poured coffee into a mug, and shook his head. "Even if there is arsenic in the tea, we have to prove Aldrich put it there."

"Who else could have done it? And it all fits. He killed Mary the same way. I'd bet my life on it!"

They were in the sheriff's office drinking Nettie's coffee, which tasted like forty-weight Penzoil. It was obvious that the sheriff wasn't convinced about the new theory.

"Is it enough to pick him up for questioning, and start an investigation?" Jennifer asked.

"Maybe, but we'll have to get a sample first, and get it tested."

"In North Platte?"

"We have a pretty good lab at the new hospital now. Maybe someday we can prove our department deserves its own lab, but until then . . . ''

"How long will it take?"

"Not long if I push it through. I'll send a patrol car to the ranch."

"A patrol car would be too conspicuous, Sheriff Cody. I'll go get the sample, but I want to call Pam first."

"And what are you going to tell her?"

"The truth."

Pam picked up after the fourth ring, and she sounded out of breath. "Sorry, but I was in the shower."

"Is your husband out on the range?" Jennifer asked.

"Yes. Has something happened?"

"You told me your tea was a special blend. How so?"

"Because Richard had it made especially for me."

"How long ago?"

"Maybe six months. He went to North Platte on business, and came home with several large boxes full of tea bags."

Jennifer took a deep breath. "Does your husband drink tea?"

"No. He's a coffee drinker."

Another deep breath. "We have reason to believe there is arsenic in the tea, Pam. Don't drink another drop. I'm on my way to pick up a sample." Jennifer heard several clicks, and a buzzing noise. "Pam, are you there? This is a terrible connection. Look, I know how you feel, but you're going to have to put your emotions on hold. We'll get the sample tested as quickly as possible, and if it's what we suspect, the sheriff will pick up your husband."

"I-I can bring the sample into town. I can take one of the trucks. Richard keeps the keys on a Peg-Board in the kitchen. I don't want to be here if . . . I don't want to be here. You said you could find a place for me to hide?"

"Yes, I can, and I think that's an excellent idea."

"Do you want me to bring just a sample, or the boxes?"

"Bring the boxes. No point in leaving behind evidence that can be destroyed."

"I'll have to pack a few things. . . . "

"No! The sooner you get out of there,

the better. Do you know how to get to the sheriff's office?''

''No.''

''Okay, then we'll meet you at the clinic.''

Jennifer hung up, and tried to calm her racing pulse. ''Did you catch most of that, Sheriff?''

Jim nodded. ''Enough to know she's on her way to town.''

''And she wants a place to hide. Those were her words, Sheriff Cody. She's scared to death.''

''What about the tea?''

''She said her husband went to North Platte on business about six months ago, and came home with several boxes of tea bags made especially for her.''

''Those the boxes you mentioned?''

''Yes. And we'd better hope this isn't the day Aldrich decides to return to the ranch early. If he finds his wife and the tea bags missing . . .'' She felt sick at the thought. ''I told her we'd meet her at the clinic. It shouldn't take her more than a half hour.''

He picked up the phone. ''You go ahead.

I have some calls to make, and I'll be there in about ten.''

Jennifer nodded, and headed for the door.

Chapter Eight

Jennifer walked into the clinic at eight-thirty, and found Ben giving Mrs. Wiggs's Dandie Dinmont terrier, Sir Scuffy, his yearly checkup and shots. Officially, the clinic didn't open on Mondays until nine-thirty, but Ben had made the exception for Mrs. Wiggs because she had an appointment at the beauty salon at ten. Ben was like that, always bending the rules, and this tendency was one of the reasons he was a good vet. He cared about the owners, as well as their pets.

Jennifer greeted Ben and Mrs. Wiggs with a smile, gave Sir Scuffy a hug, and went into the outer office. Tina wasn't due in until noon, and she was glad to have this quiet time alone. She needed to regroup her thoughts, and calm her nerves. She had talked to Pam twenty minutes ago, and expected her to arrive in just a few moments. And then? It was up to Jennifer to find the distraught woman a safe place to stay, and she didn't have many options. There was only one rooming house in town and it rarely had any vacancies. No motels, except out on Route 5 near Boodie's Roadhouse, and the hotel was undergoing renovations as an historical landmark. William "Buffalo Bill" Cody had stayed there for several weeks while his home was being built near North Platte, and supposedly he had had a clandestine meeting with Chief Crazy Horse in his room during that time. Calico hadn't been much more than an outpost in those days, full of trappers, fur traders and soldiers. It had been frontier country, and considered unfit for farming. The Homestead Act in 1862 brought the settlers, but it wasn't until the early nineteen-hundreds that the area was strengthened by irrigation, cooperatives, and conservative farming methods. Where crops couldn't be grown, cattle were raised, and towns sprouted out of the dust and made history.

Jennifer smiled, thinking about Sheriff Cody, who claimed he was a long-lost descendant of Buffalo Bill. Nobody believed him, but it was fun to pretend.

A few minutes later, Mrs. Wiggs left with Sir Scuffy, and Ben locked the front door. And when he spoke, he had a scowl on his face. "No more patients until you tell me what's going on, young lady. I saw the look on your face when you came in."

Jennifer sighed. "I don't know where to begin."

"Try starting at the beginning."

Jennifer had just about brought him up to date when the sheriff arrived, out of breath and red in the face. "Sorry I'm late," he said, "but the Wilson brothers got into a fight in front of the market, and I had to haul 'em in." He looked around. "Shouldn't Pam Aldrich be here by now?"

"Yes, and I'm getting concerned," Jennifer said. ''I was going to give it five more minutes, and then call.''

''Call her now.''

Jennifer dialed the number, waited, and hung up. ''No answer.''

''Then she's probably on her way.''

''You look like you could use a cup of coffee, Sheriff,'' Ben said.

The sheriff nodded, but his expression was grim, and Jennifer knew exactly what he was thinking. Was Pam on her way? Or had her husband come in from the range early?

When another half hour went by with no sign of Pam, Jennifer said, ''We have to go out there, Sheriff. Something must have happened.''

The sheriff pinched his eyes closed with his fingers. ''Gotta think who I can call for backup. I've got deputies scattered all over the county. Guess Manny Pressman is about the closest. I'll have him meet me there.''

''I'm going with you,'' Jennifer said, getting to her feet.

''Not a good idea, Jennifer. You're not

trained for this sort of thing, and nobody knows what we'll be walking into.''

''But Pam trusts me, and I might be able to help.'' She walked out into the waiting room, whirled around, and kicked her foot. ''Ahhhh-eeeee! And I know jujitsu, karate and kung fu.''

Her stab at humor was lost on her audience. ''Yeah, but can you still shoot a gun?'' the sheriff muttered.

''Still?'' Ben asked incredulously.

''Her daddy used to take her target practicing all the time. Well?''

''I haven't shot a gun in a long time,'' Jennifer admitted, ''but don't you suppose it's like riding a horse? You never forget.''

Ben waved a hand. ''This is crazy!''

Jennifer stood firm. ''You either take me with you, Sheriff Cody, or I'll drive out on my own.''

The sheriff sighed. ''Well, let's go, then. I have the feeling this is a losing battle.''

The sheriff had contacted Deputy Pressman on the car radio, and they were heading out of town before he said, ''You really know all that kung fooey stuff? Or were you just pulling my leg?''

"It's true. I took lessons while I was in vet school."

"They teach you stuff like that to become a vet?"

"I took private lessons. It was good training—not just for the body, but for the mind."

The sheriff grumbled something under his breath, and hit the accelerator.

"Something is bothering me," Jennifer said, when they were a mile or so from the ranch. "But like this morning, when I had that elusive *feeling,* I can't put my finger on it."

The sheriff rolled down his window. "Well, you'd better hit on it pretty soon. We'll be at the ranch in about five."

Jennifer breathed in deeply. The air was fresh, with a hint of rich soil and alfalfa. To the north, puffy clouds crested into peaks and valleys, the first sign of a summer storm. *Something somebody did? Something somebody said?* "I don't know, Sheriff, but it's right there, so close I can almost taste it."

A few minutes later, they pulled into the

gravel parking area. Sheriff Cody cut the engine. ''Looks deserted.''

''Yes, but none of the trucks are gone, and there's the Jeep and the hay truck. I counted the vehicles the last time I was here. It's a habit I got into years ago,'' Jennifer explained.

''Counting trucks?''

''Counting anything. Vehicles on the road, telephone poles, mountain peaks, stars at night, the peas on my plate . . .'' She took a deep breath. ''Now what?''

He reached out to the rack behind him, and handed her a .22 rifle. ''It's loaded. Get the feel of it in your hands, remember everything your daddy taught you, and then we're going into the house.''

Jennifer felt the smooth wooden stock, checked the safety, and nodded. ''I'm ready.''

Halfway up the walk, the sheriff muttered, ''I don't like this. It's too quiet.''

''It was quiet the last time I was here,'' Jennifer reasoned. ''They only have six ranch hands, and if they are all out on the range . . . '' She sucked in her breath. ''The front door is open.'' It wasn't open

much, only a few inches, but for some reason, it made the hair at the nape of her neck rise.

Cody unholstered his revolver, and whispered, ''I'm going in first, but stay close.''

He didn't have to worry. Jennifer planned to be his shadow.

Nothing seemed out of sorts in the living room or the dining room, but when they reached the kitchen it was obvious there had been some sort of a scuffle, or maybe it had been an intruder. Drawers and cupboards had been emptied, and the contents dumped on the floor.

''Somebody was looking for something,'' the sheriff muttered, kicking at a broken dish. ''Do you know where she keeps the tea?''

''When I was here, she filled a mug with hot water, and reached into that little pot.''

The ceramic pot was still on the counter, and the sheriff turned it over. ''It's empty. How about the boxes?''

''I have no idea. Could be that was what the intruder was after.''

''Yeah, but did he find them? We'd better check upstairs.''

With her heart in her throat, Jennifer followed Sheriff Cody up the stairs, and watched as he cleared each room along the hall. Two bedrooms, and a centrally located bathroom. When they reached the room at the end of the hall, they found the door closed.

Jennifer's heart was pounding in her ears now, as the sheriff turned the knob and motioned for her to stand back. With his gun up and extended, he opened the door.

Jennifer peered around his shoulder. The room was empty. He started to walk out, but she stopped him. "Pam's purse is on the bed. I know it might be an extra, but . . ."

It wasn't. It contained Pam's wallet, cosmetics, toothbrush, and a roll of twenty-dollar bills. "She wouldn't have gone off without this, Sheriff Cody—"

Jennifer's words were cut off by the sound of an anguished moan. The sheriff nodded toward the closet, and moved up to the door. He took a deep breath and opened it, but found only clothes and storage boxes stacked on the floor. And then they heard the sound again.

They found Pam Aldrich curled up in a little ball behind the boxes, weeping uncontrollably. Cody moved the boxes out into the room, but when he reached for her, she cringed and pulled away.

"Let me," Jennifer said, squatting down. "She's in some kind of traumatic shock. Pam, it's me, Jennifer Gray. Look at me. The sheriff is here, and you're safe now."

Pam looked at Jennifer with frightened eyes, and shook her head.

Jennifer reached out and touched her arm. "It's okay, Pam. We're here now, and only want to help you. Are you injured?"

"No . . ."

Jennifer breathed a sigh of relief. "If you'll let the sheriff help you up—"

"H-he'll kill me, too."

"The sheriff hasn't killed anyone, Pam. He's here to help you."

"No, not the sheriff."

Jennifer looked over her shoulder. "We have to get her out of the closet, Sheriff Cody."

He cleared his throat. "Give me your hand, Mrs. Aldrich, so I can get you over to the bed."

Slowly, her hand came up. It was balled into a fist, and when she opened it, tea bags fell to the floor.

"That's the way," the sheriff said. "Nice and easy."

Jennifer watched while he helped Pam to her feet, and hurried to her side. "That's it, Pam. Let us help you to the bed."

Like an obedient child, Pam walked to the bed and sat down. And then she began to rock back and forth. "I thought he was going to kill me too."

"Who?" Jennifer asked, while the sheriff picked up the tea bags and placed them on the dressing table.

"Tyler. He killed Richard and Matt Cox. It was terrible . . ."

"Is Matt Cox one of the ranch hands?" the sheriff asked.

Pam nodded.

"Where did this happen?"

"In the barn."

The sheriff scratched his head. "I've got to check this out, Jennifer, but I don't want

to leave you. If we have a killer on the loose . . .''

"Go," Jennifer said quickly. "We'll stay right here. If Tyler comes through the door—" She stopped short of saying she would shoot him, because she didn't know if she could.

After the sheriff had gone, Jennifer took Pam's hand. "Can you tell me what happened?"

Pam took a deep, shuddering breath. "I got dressed and packed everything I needed in my purse. I knew I was running late, and I was so frightened that Richard would come back before I could get away. I went downstairs to get the tea bags, realized I'd forgotten my purse, but then . . . I found Tyler in the kitchen. He had dumped everything out of the drawers and cupboards. He was like a wild man when he saw me. I-I didn't know what to do. He wanted the tea bags. I didn't know what to say. I guess I was in some kind of shock, wondering how Tyler knew about the tea bags, and then I saw Richard and Matt Cox through the window. They were riding in from the range. I screamed . . .''

She shook her head, as though to clear her mind of the horrors that followed. "Richard and Matt heard the scream, and hurried to the house. The next thing I knew, Tyler pulled me in front of him and buried a rifle barrel in my back. When Richard walked through the door, Tyler told him if he took one more step, he'd kill me. I looked out the window. Matt was running for the barn. I didn't know it then, but he was going to get a gun. When Tyler realized what was happening, he ordered us out of the house and into the barn. Matt . . . Matt came out of the little room they use as an office. He was holding a rifle, but before he could get it raised, Tyler shot him. Richard went into a rage. He called Tyler a fool for stirring up trouble, and I didn't wait to hear the rest of it. Tyler had let go of me when he shot Matt, because he needed both hands to aim the rifle. I turned and ran. I was in the kitchen when I heard the second shot. I know it was crazy, but I wasn't thinking. I took the time to grab the tea bags out of the pot on the counter, and then I ran upstairs . . ."

Pam was trembling again, her teeth chattering. Jennifer put a comforting arm around her shoulder, and told her to take a deep breath.

After a few moments, Pam went on. "I ran in here. I was frantic. I could hear somebody in the house, and I hid in the closet. I heard footsteps on the stairs—it was Tyler. He opened the closet door . . . I was sure he could hear me breathing, but he finally shut the door. I heard him mutter, 'I haven't got time for this,' and then he went downstairs. I knew he'd killed Richard, too. I don't remember much after that. I remember sobbing, and praying."

Questions popped into Jennifer's head, one after the other. "Why would Tyler be interested in the tea bags, unless . . ." She remembered the clicking sound on the line when she was talking to Pam. "Is there a phone in the office in the barn?"

"Y-yes."

"And is there an extension into the house?"

"Yes."

"Remember when I called you, I said we had a bad connection? If Tyler was listening to our conversation, then he knew what we were planning to do.''

''Why would he care, unless—''

''Unless he has been in on this with your husband from the beginning. You said your husband told Tyler he was a fool for stirring up trouble. That was an odd statement. Did he say anything else?''

Pam was rocking back and forth again. ''I don't know. Everything was happening so fast. I think he told Tyler patience was a virtue, and now, because he didn't have any, he'd screwed everything up. I think Tyler said it was Richard's fault for dragging his feet.''

''Where are the boxes of tea?''

''I put them in the truck right after I talked to you. I didn't know Tyler had stayed behind. I thought he had gone out on the range with the rest of the men.''

''Well, apparently he didn't see you, or he wouldn't have asked you about the tea bags . . .''

Jennifer's words trailed off. Somebody was coming up the stairs. She aimed the rifle at the door, held her breath, and waited.

"Whoa, it's me!" the sheriff said, walking into the room. "I'm sorry to say Matt Cox is dead, but your husband is still alive, Mrs. Aldrich." He ran a hand over his eyes, like he couldn't believe this was happening. "He's in bad shape, Jennifer. I've gotten in touch with all my deputies in the field and called for an ambulance, but everybody is at least a half hour away. He might not be able to hold on that long. I know you're not a doctor, Jennifer, but maybe you can do something. The wound is in the stomach area, and he's lost a lot of blood."

"We have a cold killer on our hands here, Sheriff, and he could be anywhere. We can't leave Pam here."

"Deputy Pressman pulled in a few minutes ago. I'll send him up."

Pam was shivering again, and Jennifer gave her a hug. "I have to try to help your husband, Pam, no matter what he's done. And you'll be safe with the deputy."

Pam nodded, but murmured, "I won't be safe anywhere until Jeb Tyler is apprehended. No one will be."

On the way to the barn, Jennifer gave the

sheriff a brief accounting of what Pam had told her, and then braced herself before following him into the barn.

Richard Aldrich had lost a lot of blood and his pulse was erratic, but he was conscious, and his eyes, though full of pain, were clear. The sheriff had applied a pressure bandage to the wound with a towel, and although it was crude and far from sanitary, the bleeding had slowed considerably.

Jennifer had such mixed emotions as she knelt down beside him, she could hardly stand it. Part of her wanted to shake him and make him suffer for everything he had put his wife through. But four little words kept swimming around in her head: *Innocent until proven guilty.* And she thought of the things Pam had told her, and the words Pam had heard the men exchange. She wanted to ask him a dozen questions, but was afraid of making his condition worse.

The sheriff, however, didn't seem to share her reservations, and spat, ''You want to tell us why Jeb Tyler ransacked your kitchen, took your wife hostage, and riddled you and Matt Cox full of holes?''

Aldrich managed to choke out, ''He was always crazy. Made my life miserable. Did he . . . is my wife okay?''

Jennifer couldn't hold back her words any longer. ''Why do you care? You've been trying to poison her for months.''

Aldrich groaned. ''I told Tyler it wouldn't work a second time. How did you find out?''

''Then you admit to killing Mary?''

''I admit to everything. I'm gonna die, so what difference does it make?''

Cody said angrily, ''You're not going to die, Aldrich. You're going to live to stand trial.''

''Why waste the taxpayers' money? I'm guilty.''

''And Tyler?'' Jennifer asked.

''He was blackmailing me. He has been for years. I-I killed my first wife . . .''

Sheriff Cody spoke up. ''Confession or not, I've got to advise you of your rights. I'm arresting you for the attempted murder of your present wife, Pam Aldrich, and that's just for starters. You have the right to remain silent—''

''You can read me all the rights you want, but that won't stop me from talking,'' Aldrich grumbled. ''You want the *real* killer, find Tyler.''

Jennifer said, ''But you said you killed your first wife . . .''

The sheriff continued on, aware that if he didn't give Aldrich the Miranda warning, Aldrich would end up a free man. ''If you decide to talk, or even make a statement, it can and will be used against you. You have the right to have an attorney present. . . .''

Jennifer waited until the sheriff was through, and said, ''So now that we all know anything you say here can and will be used against you, let's get on with it. You said you killed your first wife. Was that Addy?''

Even through the pain in his eyes, Jennifer could see the look of astonishment. ''How did you find out about Addy?''

''Was it Addy?'' she persisted.

''We were on vacation—Spirit Lake. It was the first vacation since our honeymoon. We'd gone to dinner the night before, and I caught her flirting with the waiter. She was like that—friendly with everybody. It was my problem, not hers. I was jealous. We fought that night after we got back to the cabin, and the fight continued the next morning. We were standing on the dock. We said some pretty bad things to each other. I smacked her. She fell into the water. Hit her head on the dock going in. I stood there for a minute, wondering when she was going to come up. Finally, I jumped in after her, but it was early. Barely six o'clock, and the water was dark and murky. I'm not a very good swimmer, and I couldn't find her..." He stopped, and closed his eyes.

Jennifer checked his pulse, and found it steady.

A few minutes later, he opened his eyes, and they were filled with pain. A different kind of pain. "I called the cops, but the nearest substation was miles away. They finally came and found her body. I told them what happened, and they found the bruise on her head. They called it an accident."

Jennifer said, "If you had gone in after your wife right away, you might have saved her."

"Maybe, but like I said, I wasn't a good swimmer. Tyler was staying in the cabin next to ours, and saw the whole thing. After the cops left, and they took Addy away, Tyler told me what he'd seen, how it looked to him. He said I stood on the dock staring into the water for a long time before I jumped in. Said it looked to him like the whole thing was deliberate. He also said he understood. Said he'd battered a few women around over the years, and never had any regrets."

Aldrich coughed, and tried to take a deep breath. "He . . . he knew all the right buttons to push, and I found myself telling him all about Addy and our marriage—about my life in general. He was sympathetic, understanding, and right about then, I needed a friend."

"And did you talk about money? Your money and Addy's money?"

"Yeah, and that's when the wheels started turning in his head. He said he was running from the cops in New York, and needed a place to stay. That was after I told him I had a farm in Sioux Falls, and that my parents were dead. I took him back to the farm with me, but it wasn't until after I got Addy's insurance money that I finally got my wake-up call. Tyler said that unless I gave him half the money, he'd go to the cops and tell 'em what he saw that morning on the dock. Funny thing is, I knew he wouldn't do that. He was wanted in New York. There was no way he would go to the cops. But I gave him the money anyway and let him stay on, because deep down in my heart I knew I was responsible for Addy's death, and I needed a friend . . .''

His words trailed off, and this time he slipped into unconsciousness.

Jennifer felt a stab of guilt. ''I shouldn't have pressed him like that.''

The sheriff gave her shoulder an awkward pat. ''Yeah, he was just getting to the good part. I hear sirens.''

Jennifer heard them too, and stood up. ''He'll pull through, Sheriff Cody, and then we'll get the rest of the answers. He still has to account for the deaths of two more wives.''

"Meanwhile, we have a killer at large. Any suggestions?''

"Why ask me?''

He gave her a lopsided grin. "Oh, I don't know. I guess I'm impressed by your performance today. And you didn't even have to use your kung fooey.''

"But it still doesn't explain why Richard was trying to kill me with arsenic,'' Pam said, leaning against the kitchen counter for support.

They were sitting in the kitchen, amid the broken dishes and clutter, and Jennifer had repeated everything Richard Aldrich had said. The ambulance had taken Aldrich to the hospital, the coroner had picked up Matt Cox's body, and the sheriff and his deputies were covering the entire area, using horses and all-terrain vehicles. It had been determined Tyler had stolen a horse and made his escape on horseback, and he could be anywhere. They had left one deputy at the house, and Jennifer watched him through the window pacing back and forth in the yard outside. It was easy to see he was upset because he had been left behind.

"No, but I think Richard was going to tell me just before he passed out. I guess that was my fault. I shouldn't have pushed him so hard. He had a serious wound, Pam, and needed all of his strength for survival."

"But he's going to be okay?"

"The paramedics seemed to think so. Do you still love him?"

Pam grimaced. "I want him to live so he has to face all the bad things he's done. He killed the love I had for him a long time ago, when I realized what kind of man I married. We'd only been married a few weeks when he started setting down the rules. I couldn't go into town without him. I couldn't go outside, not even to do the gardening, unless he was with me. One day he caught me talking to one of the ranch hands, and he had a fit. He hit me, and called me a flirt, and worse. And then there were all those threats. I truly believed he was capable of killing me. I was petrified of him, and yet there were times when he could be so charming—like the man I married. I have to keep remembering that, otherwise none of it makes any sense.''

Jennifer watched Pam brush away the tears, and felt her heart twist. ''It might help to remember he was a willing partner in Tyler's convoluted plot too, and that you're finally free.''

''But I'll never be free from my memories.'' Pam shook her head slowly. ''Just the thought that Tyler is still out there somewhere . . .'' She appeared to blanch at the thought.

''Yes, and he's armed and dangerous. Do you want to stay here? Or go into town?''

''Can we leave?''

''Sure we can. There is no way Tyler will be on the main road, and what are we talking about? A half hour? You can stay at my house. We have a spare bedroom. Of course, it's full of exercise equipment, but we have a roll-away cot in the garage.''

''And the boxes of tea bags?''

''The sheriff will see to it the tea is analyzed. Though that seems moot now.''

"You sound like an attorney, Miss Gray."

"Maybe it's because I'm dating an attorney. That kind of stuff can rub off on a person real fast. By the way, don't you remember that you're supposed to call me Jennifer?"

"That's a pretty name, and it suits you. You're good and kind, and . . . "

Jennifer gave Pam a warm smile. If you think *I'm* good and kind, wait until you meet my grandfather. He's the pastor of the Calico Christian Church, and looks like Santa Claus. But there's also Emma. She's our housekeeper, and—"

The shot sounded like an explosion. Pam screamed, and Jennifer ran to the window. The deputy was down on the ground, and Jeb Tyler was making his way toward the house.

Chapter Nine

Both women were nearly frantic, because they knew they wouldn't have time to make a break for it out the back door, or get upstairs to the cubbyhole in the closet. Unable to understand why the man had returned to the ranch, unless he'd never left, Pam quickly pointed to the pantry door. The pantry was small and lined with shelves filled with canned goods, but there was room to huddle together. They both were trembling, and the smell of their own fear filled their nostrils.

Scarcely breathing, they listened to his footsteps and then his words, shouted from somewhere near the living room. "I know you're here, Mrs. Aldrich, and I wish I had more time to play your game of hide-and-seek, but getting the money is more important. By the time the sheriff and his posse get back, I'll be long gone."

He was in the kitchen now, and keys jingled. It was clear he had taken a set of keys off the Peg-Board, and was going to take one of the trucks.

His footsteps receded.

"What money?" Jennifer whispered to Pam.

"In the safe in the den. Richard doesn't trust banks."

"And Tyler knows the combination?"

"He must, or he wouldn't be doing this."

Jennifer gripped the .22. "Where is the den?"

"Off the living room."

"And the safe?"

"On the wall near Richard's desk."

"When he's standing in front of the safe, will his back be to the door?"

"Oh, no, you're not thinking of—"

"I don't think he knows I'm here, Pam.

The sheriff took my Jeep. If I don't do something, Tyler's going to get away!''

"He'll kill you!"

Jennifer released the safety on the .22. "Not if I can catch him by surprise. He'll have to put his rifle down to open the safe."

Without waiting for a reply, Jennifer slipped out of the pantry and made her way to the den. Timing was everything, because if she was too late and met him coming out of the den . . . She shook her head, and inched across the living room.

The door to the den was open. Jeb Tyler was in front of the safe, working the combination. The rifle was resting against the wall to his right. He cursed, and Jennifer's heart gave a little flutter. He was having problems with the safe, and that gave her the advantage. She took another step, heard a sound behind her, and looked over her shoulder. The deputy was coming through the front door.

Wanting to bawl with relief, not only because he was alive, but because she desperately needed his help, she motioned toward the den and put a finger to her lips.

The deputy nodded, and stepped up beside her. And that was when she realized his left shoulder was saturated with blood. Jeb Tyler had made his first mistake. He should have made sure the deputy was dead. Jennifer retracted that thought immediately. Jeb Tyler had made his *final* mistake. His first mistake had been made that day at Spirit Lake.

The deputy, whose handsome face looked pale and grim, motioned for Jennifer to take one side of the door while he took the other. His service revolver was out and extended.

At the same moment the door to the safe swung open, the deputy stepped into the room. Jennifer followed just as the deputy commanded, ''Freeze, or you're a dead man!''

Instantly, Tyler reached for the rifle. The deputy's revolver coughed once, striking the man's hand. Tyler screamed and reeled. Within seconds, the deputy had the man facedown on the floor and cuffed.

Jennifer felt light-headed, and dropped to the floor. She could hear the wail of sirens in the distance, and tried to catch her breath.

The deputy looked at her and grinned. "When I decided I wasn't dead, I radioed the sheriff. You okay?"

Before Jennifer could respond, she heard the gasp from the doorway. Pam was clinging to the door frame, and her face was awash with tears. "I-I heard the shot, and I didn't know . . ."

Jennifer managed a smile. "Maybe you'd better come down here so I can give you a hug. I don't think my legs will hold me if I try to get up."

Pam sank to her knees beside Jennifer, and the women embraced. At least this part of the nightmare was over.

Jennifer could hear her grandfather and Emma arguing as she wearily made her way along the walkway, and couldn't help but smile. She was safe, she was home, and it felt wonderful. She had called Wes from the ranch to say she would be late, but she hadn't gone into details. Now she would have to explain why she looked like she'd gone through another war, and she anticipated the reaction.

They didn't disappoint her. Emma looked at her with narrowed eyes and pursed lips. "If that blood on your clothing is yours, I'm going to faint!"

"I haven't been injured," Jennifer said before her grandfather could open his mouth. "Hope you didn't hold dinner."

Wes cleared his throat. "We did, but maybe we shouldn't have. Nobody will have much of an appetite now. Just tell me you're okay, sweetheart. That's all I want to hear."

She gave him a hug. "I'm okay, honest. And to tell you the truth, I'm starved. Give me a few minutes to get cleaned up, and then I'll tell you all about it."

"I think I've heard that before," Emma muttered, as Jennifer headed for the stairs.

Fifteen minutes later, Jennifer joined them in the kitchen, and peeked in a pot on the stove. It was a rich stew, full of onions, carrots, peas, turnips, and potatoes. Nothing wrong with that, but Emma had thickened the gravy with flour, added a carton of sour cream, and the concoction was brimming with calories. But tonight, Jennifer didn't care.

"Well, at least you look better," Wes said, handing her a cup of coffee.

"Hmm, a shower can do wonders."

"You want to talk about it now? Or wait until after dinner?"

She blew her grandfather a kiss. "If I don't tell you now, you'll pick at your food."

Wes sat down at the table. "I might anyway, but I'm all ears. But let me say something first. Emma said you left bright and early this morning, and that you were acting mighty strange. She also said you asked her about that episode of *Murder She Wrote,* where the husband was poisoning his wife with arsenic. It was easy to see where you were going with that notion. You might as well have left a trail of bread crumbs. I won't deny I was worried. Sometimes hitting on the truth can be dangerous. I called the clinic about noon. Ben said you were with the sheriff, but wouldn't tell me any more than that. Well, it made me feel a little better. I spent most of the day in church, polishing the pews and praying.''

Emma sniffed. ''I even had to take him his afternoon snack.''

Jennifer sat down at the table and squeezed his hand. ''I'm sorry I worried you, Grandfather, but thanks for the prayers. I'm sure they helped. I knew when I woke up this morning I was missing something. Something really important. I didn't feel particularly well, either. Sort of headachy and shaky, out of sorts. And that's when it came to me. When I was at the ranch talking to Pam, she had a little spell. Perspiration popped up on her brow, and she began trembling. She said she had been feeling out of sorts for weeks, but that she didn't think it was serious because it came and went. I remembered Mary, and how she'd been ill for a long time, and I remembered the symptoms of arsenic poisoning when given in small doses. Both women were tea drinkers. Pam mentioned it was a special blend. I went to the sheriff, and he agreed we had to get a sample of the tea. I called Pam and explained. She said she would bring a sample to town, but never arrived. That's when the sheriff and I went out to the ranch.''

Emma gave a little gasp, and then sucked in her breath.

''Pam was okay, Emma, though she was nearly out of her mind with fear. She'd gone through a terrible experience, and we found her hiding in a closet. . . . ''

By the time Jennifer had gotten to the point in the story where the deputy shot Tyler, they were drinking coffee on the porch, while the stars twinkled in the sky. Crickets chirped, and somewhere near the pond a bullfrog croaked a song. Wes shook his head. ''And Aldrich?''

''He's in the hospital. The last I heard, he's out of surgery, and out of danger. He'll live to stand trial. I'm not sure what will happen to Tyler. He's wanted in New York on a manslaughter charge, so I suppose he'll eventually be extradited. Meanwhile, he's talking to anybody and everybody who will listen to his tale of woe. He claims Aldrich is the real bad guy, and was holding what he did in New York over *his* head. Claims he's had to work all these years for Aldrich without pay, and Aldrich even made him kill all his wives. Nobody is going to buy that, of course, but now, at least, we know most of the story.

"After Addy drowned, Aldrich sold the farm in Sioux Falls and moved to Des Moines, where he bought another ranch. That's where he met and married Estelle Miller. Lots of money there too. She's the one who fell off a bluff into the Mississippi River. He inherited a fortune, sold out, and moved on. Next stop, Calico."

"And Jeb Tyler was with him all this time?" Emma asked.

"Yes, he was, and although nobody knows who is telling the truth, I have the feeling both men are equally responsible. And the pattern is clear. When the money started to run out, it was time to kill off the current wife and move on."

"What about Mary?" Wes asked. "Why wasn't her death made to look like an accident too?"

"Tyler claims that when Aldrich married Mary, everything changed. Aldrich was afraid if Mary had an accident, it might cause suspicion. That's when Aldrich supposedly devised the plan to put arsenic in her tea. When she finally died, Aldrich received the five hundred thousand from the inheritance she'd received from her grandmother, plus a good amount of insurance. That's why the long time between wives. When the money began to run out again, he had to sell most of his cattle. And then he met Pam.''

Wes walked to the railing and looked out at the night. ''And what about Pam Aldrich? The poor woman must be devastated.''

''She is. But she's also found an inner strength she didn't know she had. She's going home to try to work things out with her family, and start over.''

''And the ranch?''

''I have no idea, but I know Pam doesn't want any part of it.''

Emma shuddered. ''We've been living with murderers in our midst for fifteen years!''

Wes turned around, and said earnestly, ''We're also living with a supersleuth, Emma. Jennifer deserves a medal.''

''For nearly getting herself killed?''

''She's made of tough stuff.''

"And she's stubborn, just like her grandfather."

Jennifer listened to them argue for a few minutes, and slipped into the house. Emma had an apple pie on the sideboard, and tonight she was going to indulge. Tomorrow would be time enough to talk to Emma about a low-calorie, fat-free diet. With everything that had happened, she hadn't had the chance to talk to Ben about Elmer Dodd's nephew in Omaha, either, or have her little talk with the mayor about the senior citizens' center. And early tomorrow morning, she was going to ride Tassie to their special place, where wildflowers grew in abundance, and lion-colored grasses rippled in the breeze. She would watch the clouds build up over the high country to the north, and thank God she was alive to enjoy this bounty of love. And tomorrow, she was going to take Willy to lunch, and thank him properly for helping her. She might even hold his hand and give him a kiss . . .

She smiled through her tears and cut into the pie. Three generous slices, with dollops of vanilla ice cream.

Tomorrow . . .